The Navigating Fox

THE NAVIGATING FOX

CHRISTOPHER ROWE

TOR PUBLISHING GROUP

NEW YORK

THE NAVIGATING FOX

Copyright © 2023 by Christopher Rowe

Cover art by Yuko Shimizu
Cover design by Christine Foltzer

A Tordotcom Book
Published by Tor Publishing Group
120 Broadway
New York, NY 10271

www.tor.com

Tor® is a registered trademark of Macmillan Publishing Group, LLC.

ISBN 978-1-250-80451-8 (ebook)
ISBN 978-1-250-80450-1 (trade paperback)

First Edition: 2023

This book is dedicated to my grandfather, Stanley Rich.
When the roll is called up yonder he'll be there.

The Navigating Fox

Primus

BETWEEN THE JOURNEYS

I DO NOT ENTER CITIES; I steal into them.

So it was on a rainy autumn day when everyone in this story was still alive.

The streets of Aquacolonia were pooled with water running off roofs and sidewalks, punctuated with manure and scat. Everywhere was mud. The city was brown and gray.

I moved among horses; dainty-footed Tellus Occidens mares and their giant, clopping cousins the Empire had sent west from across Oceanus. Some were knowledgeable and made their way unbridled. Others were voiceless and so supposedly ignorant of any cosmos wider than their senses. These latter pulled carts and wagons or were saddled and bearing humans or philosophizing apes. A worshipful aurochs, the ring in his nose an affectation, bellowed plainsongs, demanding attention to his vision of the goddess of cattle.

No one paid him any attention.

No one paid me any attention, either. Until I wanted them to.

All of us knowledgeable creatures—horse or ape, aurochs or fox—were physically indistinguishable from our voiceless counterparts.

The clockwork atop the funicular station was lit against the overcast sky and told any who glanced at it the time was midafternoon. I would miss much of the talk I intended to hear at the Sodality's hall high up the hill because I had been doing some preparation. I had read Octavia Delphina's newly published monograph at the subscription library staffed by theorizing tortoises in the forest west of the city. I knew what Octavia Delphina would say. I had my suspicions of how her auditors would receive her.

The danger on that day was to my reputation, which was already in tatters. Blame was laid in Delphina's work, blame she rested squarely on me.

So why did I board the funicular and attend the detailing of my disastrous expedition, then less than a year gone?

A more complicated question to answer than it might seem.

~

The line leading to the station split at a gilded stanchion. Humans and those knowledgeable creatures small enough to fit in cars built for humans—and capable of carrying and manipulating money—broke left. I broke right. Larger knowledgeable creatures—horses and mules, mostly—slogged up the hill on their own alongside the voiceless, who weren't afforded the convenience of public transportation.

The agent on the right side was an astute baboon who held a stylus over one of the account books of the Tally House, the treasury of Aquacolonia. The books were used to track transactions among knowledgeable creatures who could not carry purses owing to their physiologies, such tracking being a practice common throughout the Empire. Immediately in front of me in line was a calculating parrot, an interesting knowledgeable creature indeed as voiceless parrots couldn't be technically said to be voiceless—they could speak, if only in imitation of others. There were few voiceless parrots this far north other than those kept as pets by wealthy imperial grandees.

The baboon asked, "Name?"

"Galerius Adamantinus," said the parrot. He did not squawk but spoke in a mellow tenor. Another difference between knowledgeable parrots and their voiceless kin.

The baboon made a note, then asked, "Number?"

The parrot rattled off the nine digits he had been assigned by the Tally House. At the end of the week, the funicular operators would turn over their records, and a debit for the ticket would be entered against the account of Galerius Adamantinus.

The parrot fluttered over the turnstile and the baboon lazily turned it so his count would be correct. He turned and saw me. His eyes widened, but he said nothing. He made a note.

"Quintus Shu'al," I said.

The baboon nodded. He had obviously already recorded my name.

"Account number seven," I said.

Again, a simple nod.

I trotted through the stile and heard him turn it behind me.

This was the way of all my transactions in the city.

I am the only navigating fox.

❧

The limestone structure housing the Sodality of Explorers was two-thirds of the way up the slope, but the funicular made no stops on its climb. I watched the building as I approached and passed it. Oil lamps shone in amber glass, indicating the Sodality was in session.

At the summit station, I spared a glance for the paddock with the great drive cogs that moved the carriages up and down the slope. These were powered by the slow circular trudge of a voiceless mammoth, almost certainly retired from the racetracks.

A small shrine to the spirit who watches over steep

slopes, brought from the Eternal City of the peninsular empire across Oceanus, stood conspicuously by the exit. Its visage was of a human woman, but the statue's body was of a lioness, one of the many goddesses borrowed from imperial colonies. There were a few coins in the brass bowl at the effigy's feet. There was no provision for knowledgeable creatures who could not carry coins to make a token sacrifice. This was not surprising. Few knowledgeable creatures keep any cult, the common term for religious practices in the Empire, with the exception of crows. Crows are exceptions to so many of the ways of civilized society.

Then I walked down the zigzagging cobbled street, passing other marble-fronted buildings housing other sodalities. Agriculturalists, foresters, various trade guilds, all with their own effigies, all with their own doorkeepers— humans all—each of them armed with ceremonial short swords and spears.

The Sodality of Explorers was no different. I recognized the woman guarding the door, a retired militia captain. Her dark skin was the legacy of her birthplace on the savannas of the enormous continent south of the Mare Nostrum.

"Quintus," she said carefully at my approach. "I did not know you had returned to the city."

"Just today," I said, looking up at her, as I always do when speaking to humans.

"The meeting has already begun," she said. "You should wait in the solarium."

The solarium would be frigid, with cold rain flowing down the glass panes of its roof. I did not mistake the insult.

"There is no statute of the Sodality forbidding a member from entering the lecture hall tardy," I said.

This was a probe for information. Had they already ousted me in absentia? Was I too late?

The answer was apparently no, for the woman struck the paving stones with the butt end of her spear and stood aside.

The foyer was, as tradition dictated, lit by torches. No one attended them, and the tarry scent of pine burned low filled the large, chilly room.

I padded across the entryway to the doors to the auditorium, leaving behind wet and muddy footprints. I took little note of this. The floors of the Sodality's headquarters were washed daily by a family of human workers who made their way up and down the slope, working in a half-dozen shrines to learning on a loosely kept schedule.

There was a calendar between the two doorways into the auditorium. It read: 2, 10, 2635, 1909, 21. These numbers were inscribed on stone tablets set in a rack that was seen to each morning by the stewards.

The second day of the tenth month, in the 2,635th year since the founding of the Eternal City and the 1,909th year of the Empire, in the 21st year of the reign of the Empress Cossutia.

"Bless her name," I muttered, out of habit, not out of conviction. The conversations in the coffeehouses and kennels of Aquacolonia were about whether the Empress ignored the needs of the parts of the Empire farthest from the peninsula. Of special interest, of course, was this port city, alone on this side of the world and not possessed of anything like the influence of those other ports around the Mare Nostrum.

A sign made of parchment was nailed to a rosewood board below the calendar. The writing on it was in a careful hand I did not recognize.

An Appeal to the Sodality for the Censure and Expulsion of Quintus Shu'al, Navigating Fox, Entered by Octavia Delphina, Citizen, Visiting Scholar.

This is what I had come to observe.

Standing before the doors, I realized if I pushed one open to enter the auditorium, I would surely be noticed. That seemed impolitic. In fact, it seemed unwise.

I knew, though, a better way to hear what this woman from across the ocean had to say about me. Although I had read the particulars of her petition in her monograph, any orator worth her salt would expand and expound, explain and explicate. And there was the period of questions and comments to follow.

That was bound to be fascinating.

The stairways to the second story box seats were hidden behind thick tapestries at either side of the foyer. The boxes were rarely used in those days, when democratic feelings in the city erased social differences. Or at least purported to.

I took the sinister side and made my way down a corridor that would have been difficult for a human, owing to the darkness. Even my eyes, though, could not read the legend engraved in a brass plate set outside the box closest to the lectern.

I had the engraving memorized, however. This was not my first time entering this box.

HELD AGAINST THE RETURN OF THOSE LOST.

I pressed through the musty-smelling curtains at the rear of the box. The low railing at the front was supported by carved mahogany posts. I settled down, rested my head on my crossed front paws, and looked out into the auditorium.

This is what I saw.

Secundus

BETWEEN THE JOURNEYS

THERE WERE PERHAPS TWO hundred humans and knowledgeable creatures of various species gathered. There were seats for those whose anatomy allowed their use and stalls, perches, and couches for those more comfortable otherwise. The great majority were humans, dressed in an array of styles reflecting the international nature of the polis—seaport center of commerce and politics that it was.

Coal oil lamps placed at regular intervals along the walls lit the cavernous room, which was draped by worn, sagging red velvet curtains. The Sodality's headquarters were old and decrepit, and its members were, in the main, not concerned with keeping up appearances.

At the front of the chamber was a small stage, lit by footlights, with a large lectern front and center. Several chairs were lined up to the right of the lectern, these currently occupied by numerous worthies. Sander Tertius, the Sodality's human prelate, with midnight black skin and a great tangle of white beard. The twin raccoon cartographers, Loci and Foci, who numbered among my oldest acquaintances. Behind them lurked someone I did not recognize and was startled to see. A great bison cow was standing with head held low, her brown eyes blinking in the lights. She had to be knowledgeable to be in attendance, rare as that was for her kind.

And a hawk-nosed white man in priest's robes. I knew him. His presence disturbed me. To the best of my knowledge, he had never made an appearance at the Sodality. Our agreement had been I would seek *him* out upon my return, not that he would seek me. He knew this would be the first place I visited in the city, and he knew I would not miss a public excoriation of myself. Yet here he was.

Behind the lectern was my would-be prosecutor. This was the first time I'd laid eyes on Octavia Delphina, Citizen and Visiting Scholar. She had the light brown skin of those native to Anatolia but was speaking in the clipped accent affected by students trained in the city-states of the Magna Graecia archipelago nearer the imperial peninsula. Her black hair was piled high on her head in an intricate coiffure that seemed better suited to a high society salon than it did a somber meeting of scholars and explorers.

"This is Quintus Shu'al's famous claim, the one that led to the loss of the Benedictus Expedition. The so-called 'Silver Roads' only he, in all the Sower's Creation, can find and follow." She nodded to someone offstage I could not see, and a pair of porters—a human man and a garrulous gorilla—trotted out burdened with a stand holding a large map. I narrowed my eyes. I recognized the map. It had been prepared by Loci and Foci based on my journeys.

The whole southern third of the continent was detailed, with the polis we sat in at its bottom, the great gulf defined by a peninsula to the east and an isthmus to the west, both held by powerful Indigenous polities. Spreading out, especially to the west and the north, the map's features became scarcer and scarcer until there were just vague sketches indicating barrier mountains or forests that had yet to be explored by any citizen of the Empire, much less any member of the Sodality.

The principal characteristic of the map, however, was the gleaming network of silver lines overlaying the depicted territories like a spider's web. I knew those routes. I was the one who found them, after all. If "found" was the right word.

"The Roads are real!" An anonymous voice rose from somewhere in the back of the auditorium. "I've followed Quintus along them myself!"

Thus roused, the crowd began murmuring, its members talking over one another and then shouting over one another.

"You're a partisan!" This howling voice came from the front of the crowd. "You made your fortune on one of

Shu'al's expeditions!" I could not see my old rival, the clever coyote E Zhupa, but I was as familiar with his voice as I was with the bitterness in it.

I still did not know who had spoken up first—describing someone as having made their fortune by means of my guiding them along the Silver Roads was to describe over a dozen merchants and traders in Aquacolonia.

"Silence!" shouted Sander Tertius. He looked as though he wished he had a spear like the door guard's, so he might pound its shaft on the floor of the stage. As it was, his bass voice ringing through the hall was enough to settle things.

"Citizen," he said to Octavia. "Please continue."

"Thank you, learned sir," she said, nodding. She went on, as if the interruptions had not occurred. "Quintus Shu'al's reputation rests on his claims to have access to magical routes only he can navigate." There was a growling somewhere in the crowd at "magical," but she pressed on.

"The practice of magic has been forbidden by imperial decree for half a millennium." Since the alchemical process that made voiceless creatures knowledgeable was developed, she did not say, the work of a hermit scholar in Brittania legendarily associated with learned mice. "Yet this so-called navigating fox flaunts his sorcery without question? Without explanation? Without repercussion?" Her voice rose as she asked the questions.

Then she asked the most important question in my life.

"And where did Quintus Shu'al come from? Of all the foxes in the known world, he alone is knowledgeable? He could not have been born knowledgeable. So, someone *gave* him voice! But he has always refused to answer questions as regard to his origins!"

"Refused" was the wrong word. It was not as if I *could* answer those questions. It's not as if I had not done terrible things in pursuit of answers. I watched the priest intensely, ultimate instigator of those actions that he was. Would he react?

A low rumbling sounded from the stage. After a moment, I realized it was the perceptive bison's voice.

"If I may raise a point of information, Citizen?"

Octavia practically wilted. The cartographers and the priest seated before the bison woman looked to Sander Tertius. In fact, everyone in the chamber looked to him.

"Citizen Delphina, the floor is yours. Will you entertain interruption by our distinguished guest?"

Before Octavia could answer, E Zhupa howled from the front, "If we're talking about secrets, what about this one? Who is this bison? Who made her a distinguished guest?"

The coyote's various allies, strategically seated throughout the audience, shouted in support.

"Our guest has requested the opportunity to introduce herself," said Sander Tertius, his voice fairly dripping with disdain. His contempt for E Zhupa was well known, though it had never translated into any particular regard for myself I'd noticed. He continued, "If you would refer to the agenda, you will see this introduction is to follow Citizen Delphina's presentation."

"I don't mind," said Octavia Delphina. "Please, ma'am, make your point."

The bison nodded. In thanks? She did not move from her spot behind the other dignitaries, but her voice was nonetheless audible to everyone present.

"I am Walks Along Woman," she rumbled. "I am the credentialed ambassador from the Great Northern Membership. I wish to say the Silver Roads are not unknown to us, and we believe them to be naturally occurring phenomena, in no way magical."

Silence hung in the air, as if everyone expected the ambassador to clarify or further explain her point. When it became clear no such explanation was forthcoming, the entire auditorium erupted in a bedlam of bellows, shouts, screeches, and howls.

This time, Sander Tertius stood up, lifted his chair, and brought it down hard, its four legs striking the boards of the stage. There was only a slight cessation in the babble, so he did it a second time and a third time.

"I will end this session!" he shouted. "I will clear this chamber!"

Gradually, the auditorium quieted. Sander Tertius nodded at Octavia Delphina. The fire had gone out of her. She had backed away from the lectern and was looking at the map of the Silver Roads speculatively.

"I think we've heard enough." This unexpected statement came from the priest, who stood. His speaking voice was, as ever, confident and smooth. "This citizen believes the navigating fox Quintus Shu'al should be drummed from this society for reasons she has outlined. This notion is not without controversy among you learned folk. But this is just a show. The Sodality has the right to discipline its own members however it wishes, within the bounds of imperial and civic law, but there is no statutory provision forbidding anyone from leading expeditions anywhere using whatever means they *claim*" — and the stress he put on the word carried curious weight — "and there is certainly no law requiring any knowledgeable citizen to explain his own origins. The regulations regarding making voiceless creatures knowledgeable apply to those who do the making, not to those so made."

Octavia Delphina looked as if she was about to object, but the priest — a veteran orator — rolled on. "Further, it is against the bounds of propriety to make these accusations and to take actions *based* on those accusations if the accused is not present to defend himself!"

"Hear! Hear!" someone in the audience shouted, but a threatening glare from Sander Tertius managed to quell another general outburst.

"Do you rise to defend him, Holy . . ." Octavia's voice trailed off. Clearly, she did not know his name.

It was a mysterious group on stage that day. They were mysterious, even, to one another.

"I am Holy Scipio Aemilanus," said the man, sketching a bow and sweeping his arm out as if he were addressing the Empress herself. "I have the honor of serving as high priest at the Temple of the Hinge. The assembly will forgive me for the violation of protocol in making myself known in public. More importantly, if Quintus Shu'al needs a defense, I'm sure he can ably provide his own. Yes?" And he looked straight up at me.

Everyone in the auditorium turned and looked at me as well.

Well, I thought. *This is certainly interesting.*

Tertius

BETWEEN THE JOURNEYS

ONE OPTION WAS TO trot back along the second story hallway, down the steps, and straight out the entrance of the Sodality. To steal away. On any other day I might have done exactly that.

Another option was to make my way to the doors to the auditorium and push through the swinging gate built for smaller knowledgeable creatures.

I chose a third option.

First, I leapt up onto the railing and slowly turned my head, taking the time to look in the eyes of as many in attendance as would meet my gaze. At a rough estimate, half of them did. E Zhupa was among those, his cruel eyes flashing in the lamplight, fangs bared. I grinned at him and made another leap. I ran along the deep molding from which the wall hangings depended. Reaching the edge of the stage, I was presented with a dilemma.

The drop to the stage was the height of two tall human men. I could certainly make the jump, but my landing would be, at best, inelegant.

I had decided, under the circumstances, elegance was required.

Looking around, I saw the old chandelier that was lit when the governing committee of the Sodality took a meal on the stage as part of one of their interminable meetings. Whoever had last winched it up had not taken the time to clear out the candle stubs from their sconces. *Tsk-tsk*.

The fixture was raised and lowered by the simple means of a rope and pulley system, the pulley being rusted, the rope being frayed. These were, like the chandelier itself, visible from the stage but not from the auditorium.

Loci and Foci, like everyone one else, were looking up at me. I nodded at the chandelier and then the spool and brake set low on the wall stage left. The raccoons looked at me, looked at each other, and shrugged.

The two of them skittered over to the rope and threw the brake. They climbed up and clung to the rope so when the chandelier started to descend, their combined weight slowed its fall.

I sprang across the intervening space and landed amid the dangling glass beads and sconces, slowly descending from the ceiling to a point just above the lectern. The chandelier stopped.

I lighted onto the stage next to Octavia Delphina and said, projecting my voice, "Hello, Citizen. I understand you have some questions for me."

⌣

I had never thought of the membership of the Sodality as a particularly unruly bunch, but Sander Tertius had his work cut out for him keeping order that day.

"Preposterous!" shouted E Zhupa from his place at the foot of the stage, looking as if he might very well leap up next to me and make his feelings known in a way I would find entirely uncomfortable. I remain smarter, sleeker, and swifter than any coyote, but would never face one in a fair fight. I would never face *anyone* in a fair fight. The human man next to him put a restraining hand on his shoulder.

Tertius gave up on any notion of propriety. "Shut up!" he shouted at the top of his voice. "All of you shut up!" This time, when he lifted his chair, he looked as if he might be planning to throw it at someone. The glare he shot at me made me realize I was high on his list of considered targets.

"Friends! Friends!" This was Scipio Aemilanus. In the bedlam, he was reminding those present that he was, in fact, a *high* priest, and of the God of the Hinge no less— the god of places in between. The power and wealth he possessed certainly outstripped that of any mapmaking raccoons, vicious coyotes, spitting prelates, or explorers of any species present. What I was interested in was the knowledge he possessed, and I had made a devil's bargain with him to obtain it.

Beneath the shouts, I heard an odd sound, as if a boulder could chuckle. Walks Along Woman was apparently amused by the entire situation. I had an incongruous thought. A credentialed ambassador might be the social equal of a high priest.

I tucked that away for future use.

Loci and Foci climbed back down the rope and took their seats again. They had the self-satisfied look common to raccoons who had just done something against somebody's idea of the rules. I nodded thanks at them. They shrugged their little shrugs. They would add this to the list of favors they had done me, deepening my debt to them in the complicated economy they made of the smallest interactions. It pays to have raccoons as allies, so long as you pay them back.

Sander Tertius and Holy Scipio Aemilanus, between them, managed to marshal something that could not quite be described as calm in the chamber. I sat and watched the process until my whiskers twinged the way they always did when someone was behind me. I turned and looked up at Octavia Delphina.

If she had wilted under the attention of Walks Along Woman, she had rallied and recovered. Her jaw was set, and anger danced in her eyes. Her nostrils flared in a way that reminded me of the worshipful aurochs I'd passed in the street.

It occurred to me she was quite a beautiful woman, as

humans judge these things.

"You, sir," she said, "are a villain."

One of those silences that sometimes happens in large groups of people coincided with her accusation. Except for a nasty laugh from E Zhupa, the silence stretched on.

"So I understand from your pamphlet, Citizen," I replied. "The arguments are very well laid out. They would be most convincing if the premises upon which they rest were not . . . specious."

Why did this woman, whom I had never seen before, whom until the day before I had never heard of, suddenly seem so familiar? The set jaw, the angry eyes . . . there was something there.

She had not replied to me, but I found myself, quite unaccountably, rushing on. "Delphina. Delphina is not your birth name. Or, perhaps, Benedictus was not your sister's birth name?"

Cynthia Benedictus had been the principal investor and titular leader of my last expedition, the one considered an unmitigated disaster, the one prompting Octavia Delphina's monograph and her talk. It was considered such because altogether sixty souls, humans and knowledgeable creatures, had set out through the northeastern forests on the Silver Roads with me as their guide. It was considered such because only I had returned.

Quartus

BETWEEN THE JOURNEYS

WITH MY PRONOUNCEMENT, the auditorium devolved into a hundred conversations, questions, and imprecations. Sander Tertius threw up his hands and declared the agenda item under question—my drumming out—void due to Octavia's false pretenses and tabled any further business. He then adjourned the meeting. I heard him apologize to Walks Along Woman and invite her to the next meeting, scheduled for ten days' time.

It was a tradition, if one often honored in the breach, for anyone onstage during a meeting of the full Sodality to remain there until the auditorium was cleared. I found myself with the three humans, two raccoons, and one bison after the not inconsiderable time it took the raucous scholars and explorers to quit the place.

When the doors finally shut, Loci and Foci immediately went to make their exit, briefly confounded by the fact that Loci went stage left and Foci stage right. Before they could correct the problem, though, Holy Scipio Aemilanus spread his arms and his smile wide.

"Friends," he said. "If I may have but a moment of your time, I wish to offer a brief précis of the proposal soon to be delivered to each of you by courier."

I noted everyone's reactions. Calm consideration from Walks Along Woman, perhaps a bit of avarice from the twins, narrow-eyed suspicion from Octavia Delphina. Sander Tertius did not meet my eye.

He knows what this is about already, I thought.

"In brief," said the priest, "I am funding an expedition to close the gates of Hell."

Sander Tertius contemplated the empty auditorium and set a grim expression on his face. Clearly, he did not plan to be the first to respond to this wild pronouncement. Loci started to giggle, but Foci poked his brother hard in the belly. Octavia seemed confused and my normally well-schooled expression showed the same, I was sure.

Walks Along Woman said, "Do you know the way?"

I was curious what Scipio Aemilanus' answer would be. Instead of answering aloud, he looked at me. They all did.

"Do *I* know the way? To *Hell*?" There was a high note in my voice I regretted. So much for well-schooled. Scipio Aemilanus knew I did.

"You are the greatest navigator on the continent," said the Holy. "I bow to no one in my admiration for the distinguished ambassador and hope she will forgive me a slight revision of her question." He didn't wait for Walks Along Woman to respond. "Quintus Shu'al, can you *find* the way?"

"It is not my practice," I said, playing the part he apparently intended for me to play, "to die in the pursuit of my vocation."

"You don't seem to mind *others* dying as you pursue it," snapped Octavia.

I wanted to respond, but Sander Tertius said, "We are still eagerly awaiting the report Quintus will be filing, now he is finally returned to the city. Until then, Citizen Delphina, we will follow the traditions of the Sodality and the laws of the Empire and give him the benefit of the doubt."

She spat. She honestly *spat* on the pine boards of the stage, close enough to where Foci sat that he drew himself full up onto his chair and hissed at her.

"I am confident the facts will exonerate our friend, Citizen," said Scipio Aemilanus. "His reputation has remained unsullied until now, despite the rigors of the expeditions he has undertaken on behalf of this Sodality and of this city. And now, I am asking he undertake a great journey on behalf of the Empire itself."

"To Hell," rumbled Walks Along Woman. She chuckled and shifted her weight. "If you good people will excuse me, I do not believe I can make any significant contribution to this conversation."

"Please," said the priest. "A moment more of your time,

Ambassador. This *does* concern you, or I would not be sending you the full proposal."

She swung her head around to stare him up and down. She sighed. "You mean to go north," she said.

Quick-thinking, this one, I thought. I could follow the leap in logic she had made, but I would not have made it myself.

"You believe your . . . destination . . . lies in the territory of the Great Northern Membership," I said.

"More likely beyond it," said Scipio Aemilanus, and the raccoons scoffed.

"The territory of the Membership—" said Loci.

"—extends north to the ice," said Foci.

The twins were not particularly talkative. When they had something to say, though, it was inevitable they said it in chorus.

"Learned prelate," Octavia Delphina said to Sander Tertius, "did you know about this . . . this foolishness?"

Sander Tertius sighed. His answer was a bare nod.

"And why, sir," she continued, "are you giving it the stamp of your authority?"

"I am authorizing nothing!" Sander Tertius snapped, before deflating somewhat. "It is not my place to approve or disapprove of this Holy's expedition. The approvals he needs have been sent from the Eternal City itself."

The raccoons clicked at one another in some chatter that was presumably intelligible to them.

I said, "You said 'expedition.'"

"What of it?" Sander Tertius replied. I had expected his response to be annoyed. Instead, he seemed out of his depth, something I had never experienced of him.

"Not '*proposed* expedition.'"

"Ah, you are all such perspicacious people," said Scipio Aemilanus, laughing. "We will make wonderful companions of the road."

"You expect each of them to take part in this . . . in this scheme?" demanded Octavia Delphina.

The priest gave her a sad-eyed look. "It is my sincere hope to convince *you* to involve yourself in this great undertaking as well, and of your own free will," he said.

No one responded to the implicit threat.

"You, prelate, will arrange the necessary equipment and voiceless beasts of burden we will need on our quest for the gates of Hell. In addition to those present, the expedition will include members of my own order. Citizen Delphina, you will serve as the expedition's recorder and, I daresay, its conscience. As we will be following in the footsteps of your sister's party, I expect you will do well in both roles. You two adepts"—here he looked at Loci and Foci—"will map the way to the gates, and if you, Ambassador, will be so kind to accompany us to the Membership's lands and gain us rites of passage, the Empress will be in your debt."

Again, his pronouncements were met with silence. At

least until Octavia Delphina spoke. "I *will* go. But I am no one's conscience."

At that moment, she reminded me so much of her sister.

"And I am to find Hell," I said, aloud, silently adding *again*.

"You are," said Scipio Aemilanus.

"And your role is to fund this quest?"

"That is one of my roles. The least important."

"And the most important?"

A faraway look came to the wiry man's eyes. "My most important role, good navigator, is to march to the entryway to the underworld, close the gates of Hell, and end death forever."

So, this time, he was to accompany me. This time he wanted me to take *him* to Hell.

Quintus

BETWEEN THE JOURNEYS

DEATH. HELL.

The two concepts are inextricably intertwined in imperial life. Other cultures the Empire has encountered often have more complex afterlives—if they hold to the concept of an afterlife at all—envisioning paradises for the good and reserving punishing or indifferent eternal realms for others.

But every subject of the Empire, the thinking goes, is bound for Hell.

Whether Hell was a nightmare place of unending torture, a measureless gray space of spectral souls drifting for all time, or simply a vast underground space where the departed carried out echoes of their earthly lives was a matter of some debate. There were other theories as well, each espoused by groups of philosophers or, more often, Holies.

To the best of my knowledge, there was no one who believed Hell was a particularly pleasant place to spend eternity.

I was familiar with the finer particularities of how the followers of the God of the Hinge viewed the afterworld. I was aware they regarded Hell as an actual physical place accessible to the living. I knew a great deal about what those Holies believed.

I had heard Scipio Aemilanus declaim upon the subject of Hell. I had never heard him propose that finding and closing the gates of Hell would end death.

I didn't know what "ending death" might mean.

But I knew what finding the gates of Hell meant.

The plan advanced by the high priest Scipio Aemilanus—and the high priest Scipio Aemilanus was someone I was deeply and unpleasantly indebted to, and him to me—was, for me at least, unacceptable.

After his outlandish pronouncement—I overheard the twins simultaneously and nearly inaudibly breathe the word "insane"—the Holy sent us on our way with smiles and, for me, a patronizing pat on the head. Sander Tertius retreated to his chambers in the back of the Sodality's hall without speaking any further, Loci and Foci waddled out of the auditorium as fast as their legs would carry them, each casting me a baleful look as they went, and Octavia Delphina and Walks Along Woman left together, one with a light step and the other with a very heavy step indeed. I trotted past them. It is my habit not to be the first to leave a place, but not to be the last, either.

So, back out into the mud. The rain had returned and

was running down the gutters on either side of the cobbled street in paired streams. I leapt over the one fronting the Sodality and considered whether to turn uphill or down.

I had dens in both directions. I did not precisely keep a home in Aquacolonia, but whenever I found myself visiting a locale with some frequency, I arranged to have someplace to stay warm and dry. Someplace, if it came to it, to hide.

Looking up the hill, I saw Octavia and Walks Along Woman making their way in that direction, presumably to the funicular station, as the highest parts of the city were scantly built up. An ambassador, at the least, would have lodgings in one of the finer districts near the Tally House. Visiting scholars like Octavia usually stayed in one of the wayhomes near the university.

If they were going up, I was going down.

I did not bother to avoid the humans or creatures— knowledgeable or voiceless—that were making their way up from the city center or down to it. I bounded quickly among them. I dashed between the legs of horses and oxen. I leapt over carts laden with the endless supplies of food humans required when they gathered in too large a number.

All cities have too many humans.

The thought is not original to me.

The rain stopped by the time I made my way to the

temple district and took to the alleys. The den of mine secreted there was not my most comfortable. It was not even the closest I could have chosen. But it had the advantage of being in the crawl space below the Temple of the Hinge, which meant *I* had the advantage of Scipio Aemilanus.

Early in my association with the Holy, I had found the latticework vent in the foundation of the temple and pried it loose. I spent many nights scratching my way up through the floor and into a forgotten cupboard I scouted out in one of my daylight visits.

I have always found it advisable to have a means of ingress to the places of power of my enemies or allies. Or, as was the case with the Holy, someone who was both. And any means of ingress could serve as a means of egress.

Scouting the crawl space, I kept my ears tuned upwards. I knew the footfalls of everyone who frequented the temple, especially the acolytes and minor priests who lived there, serving their half-mad god of liminality. It was approaching the dinner hour, and there was a great deal of walking about in the kitchen and in the vaulted room where the clergy took their meals.

Silence came from the apartments where the high priest lived.

The forgotten cupboard was in the mudroom of the apartment, which had a separate entrance from the street that had been sealed up decades before. Not that Scipio Aemilanus would ever have used the room anyway. He wasn't one to get muddy.

He arranged for others to do so on his behalf.

So, an hour or so later, when he made his way into the wood-paneled room where he kept his papers and books spread across a great oak table surfaced with felt, I was sitting in the corner, in the dark. Dark for him, at any rate.

He did not see me until I spoke, but my speaking did not startle him.

"Pay up," I said.

My plan, such as it was, was to get what I was owed and leave the city. To steal away before I found myself leading another ill-fated journey north.

Scipio picked up a sheet of paper from the table, studied it for a handful of heartbeats, then set it back down. I caught a glimpse of what was on it, a sketch of a human woman I recognized from carvings and coinage as Empress Cossutia.

As Scipio fancied himself an artist, his messages to me over the years had often included explicatory drawings, so I assumed the sketch was his own work. But I do not have an educated enough eye for human art to distinguish individual styles, so this was merely a theory. His expression was of longing.

His stalling done, the Holy—what a word—gave me a long look.

"You have proof the sacrifice was undertaken?" he asked.

I scoffed. "Why do I need to offer proof when you already have the testimony of your other agents? I saw your cursed bird shadowing the Benedictus Expedition from the start." Then a thought. "How did she know where and when we would step off the Roads?" I was not the sole knowledgeable creature in the Holy's thrall with unique gifts, but the argute crow Malavus' were a mystery to me.

Scipio Aemilanus' private smile was decidedly more unsettling than his public. "That was not the secret you bargained for," he said.

I hesitated. I may have trembled. "You will tell me, finally."

He did not answer. He strode across the room to a cupboard equipped with a lock, one far too clever for even a nimble knowledgeable creature's fingers. Scipio turned several dials and took a key from his sleeve. He turned this once left and twice right in the mechanism.

Finally opening the cupboard, he took out a rosewood box I knew well. He did not bother closing the cupboard. He carried the box over and set it on his worktable.

"Let us just review the particulars," he said.

Scipio Aemilanus was a loathsome man. Anyone would hesitate to enter into a bargain with him if they knew his true nature. Almost anyone. I had rushed to it. He had divined the one thing I wanted above anything else: the secret of my origins.

The scrolled parchment and the reagents needed to

reveal its contents were inside the box. This would seem foolish to any unlikely thief, who might think he had stumbled across some hidden secret and the means for revealing it in the same place.

Scipio Aemilanus might be loathsome, but he was no fool. Painting the parchment with the contents of the corked clay bottles from the box would indeed clarify the hidden text—but not the text that was important.

Deeper than the misleading words that simple application would reveal—I never knew what those words were—were the terms of our agreement. The reagents *were* needed to reveal those as well. But so was a measure of the Holy's blood. So was a measure of mine.

Really, I thought the whole obfuscatory rite was an example of Scipio's paranoia. Or it may have just been an excuse for him to cut me.

"This will go easier for both of us if you hop up here on the table," he said lightly. He drew a little knife, its hand carved of illegal ivory, from one of his bottomless and bountiful sleeves.

I despised following his suggestion. But then, I despised following his orders, and was here because I'd believed following his orders was the only way I had to learn what I so desperately needed to know. What I had to learn no matter the cost to anyone.

A cut of his palm, a deeper one to the pad of my right forepaw, and the blood from both wounds was mixed into the clay bottle. Scipio took a gutta-percha brush and applied the steaming stuff to the parchment.

Words written in walnut-colored ink fought their way up out of the scroll. The text was dense, self-referential in obscure and circular ways, weighted down with the symbols and sacred logic of the Hinge God's cult, written in a cramped, spiky hand.

For all that, the substance of the bargain those obtuse words described was simple.

"You were to see to the deaths, at a time and place of my choosing, of Cynthia Benedictus and her companions," said Scipio.

"So I did," I replied. "Now you are to tell me why I am the only navigating fox."

The disturbing smile again, and I realized I would not receive the negotiated payment. He said, "Oh, dear Quintus. You never ask the right questions. The *why* is not important. You should wonder instead, who? Who made you knowledgeable? Because you were raised to consciousness by no subject of the Empress."

There are very few people, humans or knowledgeable creatures, who have ever stunned me into silence. I opened my mouth, willing myself to respond.

My will failed me.

Sextus

THE FIRST JOURNEY

IT HAS ALWAYS BEEN my opinion—and in a way, my opinion is the only one that matters—that the Silver Roads do not traverse space so much as they do time. I have discussed this before with Loci and Foci, but their interests are in practicalities, not theories, so those discussions usually ended with me talking to myself as they wandered off, one after the other.

But consider. To step onto a Silver Road is to step *out* of something else. Out of what, exactly? The world? As good an answer as any.

And the world is defined not just by the places and peoples in it, but also by the passage of time as it is experienced by those places and peoples.

To be more specific, people require time to move between places. Sometimes a short amount of time, depending on the distance between two places and the speed of the traveler. Others, a long time indeed. To travel from the funicular station at the top of the highest hill in Aquacolonia to the Sodality of Explorers at a human's brisk gait is the journey of a few moments. To travel from Aquacolonia to the first of the gates of Hell on the map supplied to Cynthia Benedictus by Scipio Aemilanus would take a very long time.

If one were to travel traditionally.

If one were not to take the Silver Roads.

Cynthia Benedictus, though, did not know she was bound for Hell, and neither did any of the sixty-odd knowledgeable creatures and humans who had joined her on her quest.

Hers was an outsized party for venturing into uncharted territory, but everything about Cynthia Benedictus was outsized. Her ridiculous mane of oiled, curly black hair that was forever full of twigs and leaves, her hips and stomach and breasts, her great round nose, and, most of all, her enormous, lustful laugh.

I enjoyed her company as much as I'd ever enjoyed that of any human. She was quick and sly, which reminded me of myself. She used humor as arms and armor both, correcting what she thought needed correcting with sharp witticisms and using ribald jokes to deflect any questions that might reveal the profound depth of her wisdom and the subtle keenness of her intellect should she answer them directly.

I have never been noted for my sense of humor. And while, yes, I am quick and sly, I would never describe myself as wise. I think Cynthia Benedictus knew all of that about me within the first few hours after we met on the Street of Provisioners, her bearing a letter of introduction from Scipio Aemilanus and me operating under secret instructions from that same man to agree—to *appear* to agree—to guide her wherever she wanted to go.

Not that where she wanted to go was specified in the plan she lay out before me. What she was seeking wasn't a place so much as it was a notion.

Cynthia was the latest of the so-called Hundred Savants to make their way across the great ocean. Since the Empress' wasting illness had been publicly acknowledged a half-dozen years prior to Cynthia's setting out on the Silver Roads, ten or twelve of the physicians, scholars, and learned adepts of various fields of study had come to Aquacolonia, taking part in the worldwide search for a cure their fellowship had been tasked with. I do not know what priest of what cult decided they must number exactly one hundred.

None of those ten or twelve had seemed particularly imaginative or ambitious. Only one of them had bothered to leave the city, and he did not make use of my services, nor those of any of my competitors. Not that they were needed for a week's journey to the nearest paramount chiefdom—the name the Empire uses for the various polities, alliances, and trade networks that makes up the larger Indigenous networks—where he was summarily turned away empty-handed.

Cynthia Benedictus, though, was not lacking in imagination or ambition. Her studies had led her to formulate a theory that certain salts and minerals characteristic of the streambeds that veined old, low mountains, such as those far northeast of Aquacolonia, might be alchemically distilled into some sort of medicine, presumably the sort of medicine which might prove efficacious for the treatment of our beloved Empress.

"You simply have to guide us to the mountains," she told me. "My colleagues and I can do the rest."

There was nothing simple about it. The heavily forested eastern mountains were the territory of Indigenous societies who could claim kinship with the human members of the Great Northern Membership, but who were no allies of the plains peoples. Since there was a pact of peace between the Empire and the Membership, they weren't friendly with the people of Aquacolonia either.

I had explored the mountains to some extent, but alone. They consisted of heavily wooded ridges and valleys, drained by thousands of creeks and streams finding their way off the eastern continental divide directly into Oceanus, and off the western into great rivers leading to the greatest river of them all, which some of the Indigenous peoples called the Father of Waters.

The more aggressive of the chiefdoms in those forested hills were known to kill imperial subjects on sight, though the appearance of a lone fox would not normally excite any interest among their roving bands of scouts. But my safety depended upon the scouts being humans. Knowledgeable creatures do not smell like their voiceless kin. A gifted nose will easily discern a navigating fox from a voiceless one.

Humans do not have keen noses. The paramount chiefdoms corrected for this shortcoming by employing the service of bounty-hunting black bears, so traveling alone, I would have to be careful off the Roads.

I explained this to Cynthia Benedictus. Not because I wanted to warn her off—I needed her expedition to go forward—but because it was important I be seen by my colleagues to be performing due diligence.

"My first tutor was an old gray bear from the steppes. He could recite epic poetry for hours without interruption," Cynthia Benedictus told me. "I like bears."

So much for due diligence.

Thus was her way, I found. I, or some other worthy of her company, would come with grave warning of dire consequences if we followed through with some action she had ordered. She would laugh it off. This laughter was not dismissal. It was an invitation to rethink things, to see opportunities and answers instead of dangerous, unanswerable questions.

Perhaps a week after we left Aquacolonia, after we had stepped off the Silver Roads for a day so the members of the expedition could recover from the exhaustion that comes over anyone who long walks them other than me, I brought up her old tutor. "These black bears are called 'quick-witted.' I do not know the appellation for a bear from the steppes."

"Would you believe me if I said they're poetical bears?" she asked.

"I would not," I said.

"Don't be so dour, Quintus," she replied. "It doesn't suit your color."

Septimus

THE SECOND JOURNEY

THREE MORNINGS AFTER MY meeting with Scipio Aemilanus in his chambers, Octavia Delphina did not evince the same zeal for exploration her sister had. We waited by the hostelry at the north side of the city for an hour before the Holy sent one of his under priests to find her. I idly sketched out an escape in my mind.

She arrived before the priest returned. Scipio's instructions to the boy had been to not return without her. Given the slavish loyalty and attention to detail Scipio demanded of the under priests, I suppose the boy is wandering Aquacolonia still, forever searching for a woman he will never find.

When she did finally arrive, Scipio immediately confronted her over the fact she had brought no baggage beyond whatever she was carrying in a small rucksack hung over one shoulder.

"You *do* realize we are undertaking a long and serious journey, do you not?" he demanded of her.

Octavia dismissed him with a wave. "I thought the

Silver Roads were supposed to be safe and preternaturally fast."

I did not know if she had somehow remained willfully ignorant of my unique ability to lead people along the Silver Roads or if she was simply taunting me. Seeking allies, I quietly put the question to Walks Along Woman, who stood nearby.

"Mockery," the ambassador said. "She knows what you claim to be capable of. Did you not read her monograph?"

"I skimmed," I said. "I'm interested in your use of the word 'claim.' I thought you said the Membership knows the Roads."

"We know *of* the roads," she said, and strode over to watch Loci and Foci attempt to load a mule with their equipment without much success, until they finally coaxed the voiceless beast to kneel. The two of *them* had certainly not stinted on gear.

Walks Along Woman had a pair of human companions looking to her needs. One was a broad-shouldered man, copper-skinned with black hair like most people Indigenous to the continent. He appeared to be an assistant to the ambassador in her official duties. He carried a beaded satchel Walks Along Woman explained held the official documents recording her visit to the city. The second human was a short woman charged with their three mules, two of which were laden with fodder—for the voiceless mules and the knowledgeable bison alike—and the third of which carried the supplies needed by the two humans.

The Great Northern Membership famously prided itself on egalitarianism, so I knew these were not servants, though whatever other name I might call them was a small quandary. As to their given names, as with so many humans who have crossed my path over the years, I do not remember them.

Scipio Aemilanus had a total of five humans and one chimpanzee in his entourage, all of them male Holies of various rank and each of them with a pack animal—mule or horse—to attend to. Only the chimpanzee had not followed his master's example in arriving in an outfit that came close to being a parody of a human explorer's typical attire. Like most knowledgeable creatures, chimpanzees did not typically wear clothing.

As the last bags and bundles were being tied to the mostly placid animals, I wandered over to Scipio. His heavy boots and oiled leather greatcoat would keep him warm and dry. Of course, there was no weather to speak of on the Silver Roads, and the temperature was steady, if cool, as in a deep cave.

"Are you setting out on travels to the wilderness or are you and your underlings preparing to stage some epic adventure in the theater?" I asked. I was tense, more on edge than I wanted to appear to be.

Scipio ignored my jibe. He was looking at the cloudy northern sky, eyes narrowed. He gave a satisfied nod.

"Here she is," he said.

I did not need to look up to know who he meant. A moment later, a large crow lit on the edge of a stone water trough, startling the twins' mule. They went to chide the bird, but saw who it was and simply sulked away, drawing their animal after them on its long lead.

This was Scipio's closest associate, the argute crow Malavus. That was not her real name, which was a closely guarded secret I never did manage to uncover. She had gifted it upon herself and, foul and unpleasant a creature as she was, no one ever suggested it did not fit.

"There is a civic patrol checking wagons for contraband at the Pine Road crossing," she said without ceremony or greeting. "You will reach them an hour after you depart." She looked around at the minor chaos of priests and raccoons wrangling pack animals. "You *do* plan to depart today, do you not?"

"We are leaving right now, in fact," said Scipio. His tone was not short, as it would have been if he had been speaking to one of his under priests. He shouted, "Get them moving, Curate!"

The chimpanzee instantly started walking from animal to animal, smacking them on the flanks. Loci and Foci hissed at him but took off after the three priests who led the way. When he reached Walks Along Woman, the curate raised his hand as if to strike her. Her attendants were on him instantly, attempting to hold his arm back.

Chimpanzees are far stronger than any human, and he flung them back. They stumbled, and came at him again. Scipio was shouting and Octavia Delphina had turned pale.

I watched.

So I saw how quickly Walks Along Woman turned, saw the blurred movement as she lowered her head, twisted it, raised it again.

The chimpanzee landed with a crash next to the water trough. Malavus laughed her hard, high laugh.

"Your explanation for this?" asked Walks Along Woman, staring down Scipio Aemilanus. To his credit, he looked aghast.

"I did not know!" protested the chimpanzee before Scipio said anything, but snapped his jaws shut at a murderous glance from the high priest.

"He will not be accompanying us, honored Ambassador," said Scipio, absent his usual smoothness. To the disgraced curate, he said, "Return to the temple and have the lowest ranked Holy present administer one hundred lashes to your shaved back. Then nothing but water for ten days. Do you understand these instructions?"

The chimpanzee raised no protest. He merely nodded and loped off into the city.

"I did not mean to inquire as to an explanation for your priest's behavior, Scipio," said Walks Along Woman. "I meant to inquire as to why you had not told him who and what I am."

Scipio bristled. "It is not the practice of a high priest of the God of the Hinge to inform inferior priests of anything they do not need to know."

Walks Along Woman looked at the man I assumed was her courier. He said the only words I ever heard him say. "Your inferiors need to know that to strike a member of the ruling council of the Great Northern Membership is to face immediate execution. We were not simply trying to prevent him from hitting the honored bison. We were trying to save his life."

Scipio had no answer.

"I believe we were just going," I said.

Octavus

THE SECOND JOURNEY

THE MERCHANTS AND OTHERS who usually hired me were satisfied by my explanation that the entrance to the Silver Roads they sought leading north into the heart of the continent lay north of Aquacolonia. On the other hand, they found it perplexing that the Roads leading east begin west of the city and those leading west begin to the east. The Silver Roads leading south actually begin in a dockside warehouse owned by a curious cat and her many offspring, but the roads leading south lead into the sea.

I well knew the network of northbound Silver Roads spread out like a web woven by a drunken spider. The entry point was at a crossroads of a stone imperial road running east-west along a small river and a road I alone could see—unless I led others onto it.

A light rain returned as we made our way to the crossroads. Everyone bore the chilly drizzle stoically except for our leader, Scipio Aemilanus. He voiced a litany of complaints as we walked.

Why couldn't we ride the horses? Walks Along Woman

gave him a contemptuous look as I answered. Voiceless riding horses were easily spooked by the unpredictable sounds that could ring out on the Roads. We would have trouble enough with the animals we had brought, though in the case of the horses, at least, I had arranged for animals their sellers claimed were hard of hearing. This would normally have lowered the prices I paid for the beasts, but the horse merchants of Aquacolonia knew my needs and habitually charged more for deafened animals.

I didn't mind. It was Scipio's money.

Why couldn't he have ridden in a palanquin? Because walking the Silver Roads, while faster and safer than terrestrial routes, quickly tired humans and creatures born both knowledgeable and voiceless, and his bearers wouldn't have lasted long. As it was, we would require long rest stops starting midafternoon, instead of walking long enough to camp in the evenings.

I was the only exception to this exhaustion. I did not know why.

Why not just stop and make camp on the Roads instead of stepping off them? The mists to either side were impenetrable. And no one can sleep for long on the Silver Roads, no matter how exhausted they become. Not even me. Nightmares of horrific intensity were inevitable, drawing on details of the dreamers' most private secrets.

Scipio Aemilanus should have known the answers to those questions and more. I had endured the interrogations of his secretaries more than once, giving what I thought were clear answers, if not completely honest ones, as they scratched their pens across parchments I had always assumed eventually crossed the Holy's worktable. Maybe even that of the Empress herself.

Perhaps my assumption was wrong, or perhaps Scipio Aemilanus just liked to complain when he was discomfited. Perhaps both of those things were true.

~

We stopped just short of a narrow bridge at a shallow bend in the little river. There was a ford there where ranchers drove cattle south to the city instead of trying to herd them across the stone span, which would have accommodated no more than two aurochs walking side by side. Aurochs, voiceless or knowledgeable, were not known for their cooperative nature.

"Right here," said Malavus, landing on an abutment of the bridge. "This is where he always disappears."

As usual, the crow ignored my presence, talking as if I were not there. I preferred it that way.

"A bridge to another world?" asked Scipio. "There's poetry in that."

"The Roads open at the halfway point of the ford," I said. "I am afraid you are going to have to get your feet wet, Holy."

Loci or Foci giggled. They had been on the Roads before, and there was never a raccoon who minded splashing
about a bit.

Octavia Delphina was standing nearby. She wore a look
haunted by something. Doubt, perhaps. A high priest of
the God of the Hinge and an official of the Great Northern
Membership apparently so powerful she could casually
murder anyone who offered her offense without repercussion were each taking this next step of our journey seri-
ously. If Octavia still did not believe in the Silver Roads,
she was being faced with counterevidence in the form of
those two very serious character witnesses.

"Now what?" asked Scipio. "You chant a spell? We wait
for the moonrise so the light from the water can reflect in
those strange eyes of yours?"

"We just go," the twins chimed.

"You just go," echoed the crow.

I looked around at the humans, mules, horses, and raccoons, at the bison I hoped I could trust and the crow I
knew I could not.

I said nothing. Instead, I remembered.

~

Imagine a fox.

Imagine the fox is you.

Imagine you are walking carefully down a smooth,

featureless pathway the color of the edges of thunderclouds.

There is nothing to see to the left or right beyond a whirling mist lit by a diffuse illumination with no source you can discern.

You know you are the only person on the road. You know you can step off it at any point into a wider, more real world, one full of color and life.

Imagine realizing you have been walking this road for longer than you can remember. Imagine it startles you when you realize you have a name, Quintus, and that you have a place, the wilderness of a continent lately invaded by people—humans who had created you for some purpose that is a mystery to you.

You step off the road onto a grassy hillside rising above a forest. Two human women with straight black hair braided behind their necks are waiting for you. They are dressed all in white.

"I remember my name," you say to them.

"What you remember is not your name," says one of the women. You believe her to be the older of the two.

"What are your names?" I ask.

"I was the Lady of Toosa," says the older woman. "You will never know me."

"I am the Lady of Toosa," says the younger woman. "You will come to know me."

"This is the real world," you say.

The younger woman laughs, delighted. "For us," she says. "For now. Not for you."

"Where did I come from?" you ask.

"Poor fox," says the older one. "You always ask the wrong questions."

The younger, still smiling, holds her hand out for you to sniff. She smells safe.

"It's not where you come from which matters," she says, "but where you are going."

"Where am I going?" you ask.

"For now, you are going to a place called Aquacolonia. You will be welcomed, after a fashion. Eventually. You will leave there again and again."

The older one harrumphs.

"Will you be there?" you ask.

"We will be here," says the younger woman.

The older puts her hand across the younger woman's. She smells wise, but not safe. "Maybe later," she says. "We may be here later."

"I do not understand," you say.

"That is your way," she says. She sounds wise, but not safe.

"My way is not to understand?" you ask. The implications of your own question frighten you.

"Your way is the way of the fox," the older woman answers.

"Foxes don't understand?"

"They never did before," she says.

Imagine you are me.

Imagine this is all you remember of your origins, all you remember before stepping off the Silver Roads into a shallow ford and looking to the south where you see a city of limestone and timber.

Imagine knowing this is not your home.

Imagine you are a fox who has no home.

~

Scipio had spent our morning travels playing a fool to the rest of them, and I did not know why. He knew about the ford, unless he had somehow forgotten about it from the numerous reports I had provided, and which Malavus had clearly confirmed.

I had never known Scipio to forget anything.

I wondered if this information was of any particular use to me. Since he had deflected and deferred after he had produced our contract back at the temple, since his promise all would be revealed once we had reached our destination, I had avoided thinking about what I would do if he did not keep his promise.

But Scipio Aemilanus always kept his promises, if often not in the way those promised had thought he would.

"Well," said Octavia unexpectedly. "Let's just go." She splashed out into the shallows, stopped, and turned to look at me. "But I suppose we have to follow *you*." A lot of venom in that "you."

Loci and Foci led their mule around her, coaxing it a few steps. They paused as mists conjured by my will rose from the river. The cloud thickened so quickly it obscured the far shore but the mists did not spill onto the southern bank. The twins disappeared into the roiling boil of vapor, their mule behind them.

Octavia watched this carefully. The expression on her face when she turned back to stare at me was just as careful.

"Actually, I go last," I said.

Walks Along Woman's two companions went next, the human woman keeping her hand near the knife at her belt. The bison followed, pausing long enough to say, "In the stories, it's always through the smoke rising from a burned patch of tall grass after a lightning strike."

"I would like to hear those stories," I said.

She nodded. "I know someone who could tell them to you," she said, and entered the Silver Roads. "Perhaps some other journey."

The under priests hesitated on the bank. Two or three of them were whispering prayers or imprecations, their voices competing with the water running over the rocks of the ford bed.

"Come on, damn you," Scipio ordered. But he did not wait to see if they followed.

Finally, it was just the priests, the scholar who despised me, and myself. "You know," I told the young men, "he can't come back without my guiding him. You can always return to the city."

They looked at one another, hesitation on more than one face. Then one of them, who had the ghost of a ginger mustache crawling across his upper lip, said, "You are wrong, fox. He would find a way back."

So they went, too.

I had forgotten the last member of our party. Malavus fluttered down from her perch on the bridge. "What will he say, I wonder," she said, "when they tell him you tried to convince them to stay?"

I pointed my nose out into the river. "Go on, if you're going," I said.

"Oh no, Quintus," she said. "That's your way, not mine." And she leapt into the air with a rustle of black wings.

"You don't have many friends, do you, Explorer Shu'al?" Octavia Delphina asked me.

I cocked my head, pretending to think about it. "I haven't noticed you have many yourself," I said.

"I guess friendship isn't my way *or* yours," she said. She sloshed through the shallows and onto the Silver Roads.

I considered abandoning them all. But I followed.

Nonus

THE SECOND JOURNEY

OCTAVIA DELPHINA'S ATTITUDE underwent a complete transformation once we had joined the others, who had lined themselves up to wait. She followed me to the head of the group.

In my experience, most people could walk along the Silver Roads for about six hours before exhaustion overcame them. There were the odd exceptions. Among voiceless animals, mules could be depended upon to keep moving as long as I had ever insisted a party keep moving, and they did not complain. I once led a pair of men who came from beyond the eastern fringes of the Empire and who used the services of a recognizing dromedary with a filthy sense of humor as a translator. The two of them stopped every two hours or so to sit back-to-back, cross-legged, and meditate. After a short time, they arose seemingly as fresh as if they had just woken from a restful night's sleep. I would have been interested to see how long they could have walked, but their cheerful and foulmouthed companion did not enjoy their unusual stamina.

I began to wonder if Octavia was like the two men, minus the meditation. She let forth an endless stream of questions and observations. She had seemingly put aside—perhaps pushed down—her blaming of me for her sister's death. Luckily, she sometimes drifted back to quiz the twins on how they had mapped the roads with no way to discern direction, location, or time.

That was an easy enough one for them to answer. They had asked me.

This did not satisfy her.

"Which way are we going?" she demanded of me.

I resisted the urge to say "straight." There are no curves or turns on the roads, just the occasional crossroad. But I relented.

"We are headed a few points west of true north," I told her.

"How do you know that?" Octavia Delphina asked.

"I have been this way many times."

This did not satisfy her, either. "The first time you were on this road, how did you know you were going north?"

"The first time I was on this road, I was going south," I said. "A few points east of south."

"Do not be obtuse, Shu'al," she said, biting out the words. "Your compatriots may have seen fit not to hold you responsible for what happened to"— she faltered—"to what happened to your last group. But I will learn the truth, and if you led my sister to her death there is nothing any guild chief or high priest can do to save you."

I raised my eyebrows. This was a softening of her stance. There had been no room for "ifs" in her monograph or in her abortive presentation to the Sodality.

"He's not a guild chief," I said.

"What?"

I had defused her.

"Sander Tertius is not a guild chief. The Sodality is not a guild. The dyers and weavers and fishers and so forth are very particular about what sorts of associations they'll let be called guilds. Sodalities are, well, they're memberships, after a fashion. Alliances of those with common interests, whether those be political, social, or scientific."

Octavia looked baffled. "Why should I care about local naming customs?" she asked.

"When it comes to annoying a dyer, you probably shouldn't. Unless you are engaged in some contract negotiation involving the dying of cloth and, forgive me if this is not the case, that hardly seems your area of expertise."

"What do you know about my areas of expertise?" she demanded.

"Well," I admitted, "beyond the fact you are a better

than average polemicist, not very much. But you should still be careful about what words you use."

"Because I might offend a guildsman?" Her tone made it less a question than a dismissal.

"Because you might offend a chief," I said.

Now she looked contemplative. "The local governments," she said. "The paramount chiefdoms and fraternities and membership and sororities. They use 'chief' to mean executive."

"I suppose some of them might," I said. "It's best not to paint with too broad a brush when you think about the people who live away from Aquacolonia and its outlying districts. If anything, their ways of life are more complicated than ours."

"So, I shouldn't use the word 'chief,'" said Octavia.

"You should use it when it is appropriate to do so," I said.

"And how do I know when it is appropriate?" she asked.

"Generally, either you ask or you are told," I said.

A voice came from behind us. "I'm a chief." It was the woman leading Walks Along Woman's mules.

I hoped Octavia wouldn't do anything more than politely acknowledge the declaration.

"That's wonderful," said Octavia.

I winced, afraid she would go on.

She went on.

"Were you born into your position?"

Walks Along Woman, who, I must say, was doing a great credit to her name, chuckled. Her companion said, "Lottery."

"You won the right to call yourself a chief in a game of chance?" Octavia sounded incredulous. Which I suppose was not particularly surprising coming from someone who had grown up in the heart of an empire where matters of politics were never left to chance.

"I wouldn't say I won," said the woman, giving the rein of the mules a shake.

"You find your duties onerous?" asked Octavia.

This time, Walks Along Woman's laugh was loud. Some of the horses farther back down the line skittered, their iron-shod feet clattering.

"Well," said Walks Along Woman's companion, "I found that my duties led me here." It was clear Octavia could tell that was the last the woman had to say on the matter.

That woman, but not Octavia.

"Are you a chief, Ambassador?" she asked Walks Along Woman.

"I was when I was barely more than a calf," Walks Along Woman said. She sounded more in the mood for conversation than her companion had. "I'm not anymore."

"You won a lottery?"

"No," said the bison. "A band of humans from the western mountains came down intent on a hunt. They startled many of my herd and meant to drive us over a cliffside, so as to harvest our broken bodies. I knew the ground and raced to the front, where the grandfathers were charging, thoughtless, heedless of any danger. I never ran so fast as I did that day."

"They sing songs about it," said the woman who had won her title in a lottery.

Walks Along Woman took the interruption in stride. "Not very good ones," she said. "But what happened was that I turned the herd. Just a few of us were taken, and those mostly the weak and slow."

Octavia said, "I cannot believe there are men who would murder knowledgeable creatures wholesale."

"Ah," said Walks Along Woman. "The herd I was born into was not made up of knowledgeable bison."

My ears pricked up.

"You lived among voiceless kin of yours?" Octavia asked, startled.

"We do not use that word," said Walks Along Woman. "But yes. When I turned the herd, I was what you call voiceless myself."

The only sounds up and down the line now were the footfalls of the horses and the mules. I looked around to see that Scipio Aemilanus had worked his way forward. He was walking beside Loci, who was perched atop the baggage on the twins' mule while his brother carried its lead. Scipio was clearly listening to the conversation between the two women as closely as I was.

"You . . . you remember being voiceless. I'm sorry, I did not know that was possible. And I do not know the word you use," said Octavia.

"I do remember," said Walks Along Woman. "And the word we use is young."

Decimus

IT IS COMMONLY ACCEPTED that knowledgeable creatures are not born, they are made. Even those who can
trace lineages, fathers and daughters, mothers and sons
who are all knowledgeable are nevertheless dependent on
the intercession of human alchemists.

The curious cat warehouse owner in Aquacolonia had
paid a small fortune to have her entire litter given voice
(with no help, scandalously, from the sailing tom who had
got them on her).

In fact, it was a cat who may have been the first knowledgeable creature. The records have long been suppressed
by the Empire, but it is generally believed an alchemist
in the islands in the north of the old world gave voice to
a cat named Nox three hundred or four hundred or five
hundred years ago, depending upon which account you
believe.

The accounts are complicated by the inclusion in them
that the human was partnered in his effort by a learned
mouse named Xerxes. But learned mice claim not to have

been made knowledgeable by humans, and none in the Empire dared speak otherwise, because of their legendary skills with blackmail and spycraft.

Five hundred years seems unlikely on the one hand, because that was before the Empire's first contact with this continent. But, on the other hand, there is no place in the world where so many knowledgeable creatures live largely separate from human society.

The theories of the priests generally agree that there must have been some parallel and nearly simultaneous invention of the technique for giving animals voices across the sea—where a single scholar (perhaps with the aid of a mouse) supposedly devised the technique—and here, where a more diffuse propagation of the method or methods was proposed.

Proposed by worthies of the Empire, that is. The knowledgeable creatures and humans of this new world seemed as incurious about the question as they were close-mouthed about it.

All of which is to say Walks Along Woman's story of her youth was, so far as I knew, an unprecedented revelation. The intense, hungry look on Scipio's face confirmed for me that any such information about the Great Northern Membership was as much news to the priests of the Hinge God as it was to me.

So, while I expected the Holy to step up with his own questions, and while I was wildly curious myself, we each, for our own reasons—mine was that I generally preferred to let secrets reveal themselves, though I could not guess his—let Octavia Delphina carry the conversation.

"In the Empire," said Octavia, "creatures are made knowledgeable not long after they are born."

"We know this," said Walks Along Woman.

"The alchemists say the process is less traumatic that way. In fact, it is illegal to give voice to an animal old enough to live independently, or at least old enough to father or birth children. It depends upon the creature. There are different rules for different species in the Empire."

"Thus, no knowledgeable fish," said Walks Along Woman. "Nor snakes nor insects, nor any other of a hundred thousand types of creatures who would never be given voice under your laws."

"*Would* be?" I couldn't help myself. "They *can't* be. The process does not work on such creatures."

"I know you believe that," said Walks Along Woman.

"He believes it because it is true," said Scipio Aemilanus. "It's the law of the Empire *and* the law of nature." He sounded just this side of anger.

"Did you know catfish can grow as large as an aurochs bull?" asked Walks Along Woman.

This was clearly not meant to be a non sequitur. The mood suddenly felt dangerous. Somehow, without me noticing, we had come to a halt.

I felt that whoever spoke next would dictate the flow of a conversation which seemed curiously . . . planned. Walks Along Woman was as powerful and high-ranking a knowledgeable creature from the outlands known to Aquacolonia as had ever had regular contact with the Empire. This was a gambit.

I did not want to speak next. But that left either the manipulative priest or the feckless young scholar.

"I have heard," I said, "there are fish in the sea who are as large as houses."

Walks Along Woman took a few steps. Behind her, the twins urged their mule to follow along, and the whole train began moving again, if at a slower pace.

"I would like to meet such a fish," said the bison.

"I would like to meet a catfish as big as a bull aurochs," I said.

"You would not," said Walks Along Woman. "One would think you a tasty morsel."

I managed to let that pass without a shudder.

"Loci," I said to the brother atop the mule, "you've never shown me a map with a river large enough to sustain such a prodigious creature."

"I'm Foci," he responded easily.

"Well," I said, "you haven't either."

"Just because we haven't mapped a river doesn't mean there's not a river there. Maps are, by definition, always incomplete."

"And raccoons," I said dryly, "are, by definition, always cagey."

"And foxes always deceptive," said the twin on the road, who, despite what his brother had said, I was sure was Foci. Loci smelled like ink; Foci smelled like paper.

"How many foxes have you known that you can say such a thing?" This was, surprisingly, Walks Along Woman.

"One is enough." The twins chittered in amusement.

Scipio, though, was not amused. "You are suggesting, madam," he said, "that lore we of the Empire have shared with you in good faith is incomplete, or you have expanded on it in some way and left us in ignorance."

"I am suggesting, Holy," said Walks Along Woman, "that I have seen some very large catfish."

"So they were not knowledgeable?" he demanded.

"I would say they are wise," she responded.

The followers of the God of the Hinge owe their power and influence to the fact that their theology hews closely to the orthodoxy of imperial custom and law. Or perhaps it is the other way around. There is no practical difference.

It was the official policy of both bodies that the process for giving animals voice had crossed the ocean with some early explorer who had left no record. The fact there was no evidence for the theory was met with arguments based on obscure philosophical pronouncements about fallacious heresies.

I did not believe at the time this momentous conversation was taking place that my own ignorance of my beginnings could be said to be official.

I do not know why I believed that. As with everything else about my origin, there was no evidence.

Undecimus

THE FIRST JOURNEY

ON THE THIRD DAY of a journey along the Silver Roads, unless I was traveling alone, it was my usual practice to halt for a full day. The typical order of events was that I would make a rough guess as to our terrestrial position and time of day, then leave the party for an hour or two as I stepped off the Roads and had a look around.

Cynthia Benedictus, when we had reached that point on her expedition, was having nothing to do with any of that.

"I'm coming with you," she announced cheerfully, as if she had just given me a longed-for gift.

"You are not," I said.

"I am paying you," she said.

"You are paying me to keep you alive," I said.

"There is no such clause in our contract. You are a navigator, not a bodyguard."

This struck me like a blow, so much so I conceded. When I stepped off the Roads into the cattails at the junction of a creek and river, she was with me.

I knew instantly I had made a mistake.

A longboat was making the turn from the river into the creek. Had I been alone, I would have simply lain down among the reeds and watched.

"Get down, please," I said quietly.

Cynthia Benedictus had seen the boat before I had, apparently, because when I looked over, she was already crouching below the feathery tops of the stalks. Unfortunately, a human woman ducking to hide is easier to spot than a fox lying down. Under the circumstances, it was the cause of much excitement.

The men rowing the boat tacked toward us, and two others stood and called out. I speak many of the languages of the various nations beyond the borders of Aquacolonia, but I did not understand what they were saying.

"We should stand up," said Cynthia Benedictus.

"You can understand them?" I asked, surprised.

"What else would they be saying?"

Fair point.

She stood, holding her arms wide in what imperial subjects think of as a universal pose communicating peaceful intentions. I had long since learned there is nothing about peace that is universal, but in this case the people on the boat did not shoot Cynthia Benedictus full of arrows.

The two men standing in the boat leapt into the shallows and climbed the muddy bank in a manner that indicated they were long used to taking such actions. They wore the woven cotton trousers and open vests common among the people of the southeastern paramount chiefdoms. One, the shorter, had a necklace of freshwater pearls around his neck.

He smiled awkwardly, as if it was something he had not learned to do until recently, and uttered a series of fluid words plainly and clearly including "Aquacolonia."

Cynthia Benedictus looked down at me and asked, "You don't know this language?"

"I know several languages much like it," I said. "But the particulars are what get you in trouble."

"Which other language are you most comfortable speaking?" asked the taller man in the common tongue of the Empire.

Cynthia laughed that laugh of hers. The man who had spoken joined her.

He said, "I have never known a fox that could speak any language of humans. But I have heard of one."

"I have traveled this way before," I said. "I thought this was an empty quarter."

"It has been. It will be again. But a long time ago, people came here and raised a mound. The chief of all our chiefs is coming to sit atop it and consider the needs of her people."

I considered what I knew of the area. We were along the line of elevation change which marked where rivers flowing from the mountains take sudden rushing drops on their paths to the great ocean. "The chief of all your chiefs," I asked, "is she a great woman clothed in white?"

"You have seen her?" asked the man.

And that is when I knew we would shortly be honored guests of the Lady of Toosa.

Yes. I had made a mistake.

~

The history of governance in the Empire is a history of tyranny interrupted by brief periods of benevolence or anarchy. None of the three were ever entirely free of ineptitude.

The reign of the Empress I had been born into and presumably come to awareness during could hardly be said to be remarkable in any way. If the woman with supposed powers of life and death over millions of humans and knowledgeable creatures in a network of polities encompassing much of the old world could not be said to be particularly energetic, there was no one complaining. Hers was said to be a distant sort of rule even in those parts of the Empire not nearly so far from the Eternal City as Aquacolonia.

If one must live under a hereditary despot, it is best if the despot is uninterested in governance.

This left innumerable opportunities for the Empress' hands-off approach to be exploited by people—almost all of whom were humans—to apply their own hands firmly. Soldiers, merchants, priests, consuls, ambassadors, politicians of every kind, and even scholars and philosophers happily fed at the trough filled by *lack*. Lack of leadership? Perhaps. But it could hardly be said the common citizen or subject was particularly *wanting* for leadership. Most would say they could get along very well without the regulations and taxes that leadership seemed inevitably to impose. How roads and sewers would miraculously spring into existence, to say nothing of trade networks and currency, literacy or public safety, those were questions that went unanswered because they generally went unasked.

These things deeply complicate Aquacolonia's relationships with the various social and political networks surrounding its holdings on three sides. With something recognizable as a ruling council and something the Empire at least referred to as a diplomatic corps, the Great Northern Membership is the closest thing on the continent to the kinds of sovereign states existing in most of the lands around the middle sea.

To the west, the Indigenous peoples range from a polyglot mixture of mountain-dwelling aesthetes who rarely spend more than a season in one place, to several polities in the drylands whose traditions and material culture suggest they are far older than the Empire.

What most of the people the Empire encountered

on the continent shared—this is not true of the relatively unknown but definitely hostile peoples far to the south—is an apparent lack of impulse toward *acquisition.*

This is the context. But the many peoples the Empire had encountered in the new world showed an almost incomprehensible diversity.

The diplomats and ethnographers of the Empire had grown used to being confused. But there was confusion, which at least shares something with context, and there was the Lady of Toosa.

These are some of the questions that had been asked about the woman—or perhaps it was a coterie of women or a series of women, all of whom went by the same appellation.

Was Toosa a place?

If so, was it a center of political, economic, or religious power?

Were the people who claimed to be beholden to her to be properly understood as her "subjects"?

Could the Lady, should she ever exhibit a desire to do so, wield military powers?

How large were her holdings if she could be said to possess holdings?

How many towns and villages were part of the polity she controlled, if there was such a polity, and if she could be said to control it?

Who was she?

Where was she?

How much, how long, how extensive, how powerful, how influential, how rich, how hungry, how worshipful, how worshipped, how? How was the Lady of Toosa?

What was she?

The worthies who governed Aquacolonia had been struggling to uncover answers to these questions on behalf of the Empire for nearly two centuries.

The people who could absolutely be said to live in the area where she ruled universally met such questions with shrugs. Sometimes they laughed as well.

She was a great conundrum, which meant she was a great threat.

I had known her nearly my entire life.

I loved her very much.

The last time I had seen her, she drove me away from what I had thought of as my home and ordered me killed should I ever return.

~

"Perhaps she's forgiven you," said Cynthia Benedictus.

"Why would she do that?" I asked.

The whole party had stepped off the Roads. The people in the canoe had politely held Cynthia hostage as I saw to that.

The two groups were negotiating their lack of a shared language—in most cases, anyway—by engaging in some sort of contest involving several stripped branches set parallel to one another which were rolled back and forth between members of three teams made up of imperials and indigenes both. There was a great deal of laughter involved. I didn't bother to puzzle it out but sat watching the game silently in the hope Cynthia Benedictus would drop her line of inquiry.

"What did you do, anyway?" she asked.

I sighed. "I didn't say I did anything."

"You have just ignored the chance to say you *didn't* do anything in favor of saying that you didn't *say* you did anything, which means you *did* something."

There was something unassailable about that, but I didn't think it was logic.

"Everyone is doing something all the time," I said. "Even doing nothing is doing something."

"Been reading philosophy, have you?" she replied. She replied *cheerfully* I should say, and then stop saying to avoid endless repetition.

"I sometimes do fieldwork for philosophers," I said. "It's useful to keep up."

"I'm fairly sure the idea of nothing being something was introduced to the Empire from the subcontinent about a thousand years ago," said Cynthia Benedictus. "I'm not sure knowing that can be said to be keeping up."

I decided on an attempt at distraction. "What are they doing?" I asked curtly, indicating the gangs of laughing stick rollers.

"They are not killing one another," she answered. "Isn't it wonderful?"

She had a point.

The man who could speak the language of the Empire had insisted we call him Blue, though he demurred when Cynthia Benedictus asked if he meant Blue was his name. He walked up the bank to where we were sitting. He was chortling and sweaty.

"How are things going down there?" Cynthia asked him.

"I do not know," he said.

"Which side is winning?" I asked him.

"I do not know that, either, for sure," he said. "Probably not yours, though."

"I don't have a side," I said.

Blue shot a curious look at Cynthia Benedictus. "How long have you known this fox?" he asked.

"I can't say I *know* him at all," she said. "I hired him about two months ago."

"I like that word," Blue said. "Month. I like counting time like you do."

I suppose an ethnographer would have at that point asked the man how he had counted time before being introduced to the idea of months. Neither Cynthia

Benedictus nor I were ethnographers. In any event, we could not have asked because it was at that point twenty longboats carrying dozens of armed humans and a dozen growling black bears appeared on the river.

Duodecimus

THE SECOND JOURNEY

WALKS ALONG WOMAN REFUSED to travel farther when it became clear the horses of the Holies were approaching fatigue. Scipio Aemilanus insisted they were merely shirking and argued that we continue. The ambassador asked, "Quintus?"

"I'm stopping for the day," I said. "Anyone who wants to stay on the Road is welcome to. Perhaps the God of the Hinge will guide you. I've never seen any sign of a god on the Roads, though."

This stung Scipio because roads and travel were purportedly part of his god's portfolio of interests.

I paused and sniffed the air off the road, and nodded at the others to step into the natural world. We were at a place I had been many times, a copse of cottonwoods along an oxbow lake separated from a river beyond the next ridge by some ancient calamity. It was late afternoon.

The under priests and Walks Along Woman's companions began unburdening the horses and mules—Loci and Foci bribed one of the northerners with a piece of silver to take care of their mount—and Scipio Aemilanus took a seat on a camp chair that a diffident boy unfolded for him. "Will you light a fire?" he asked me.

"Alas," I said. "I have no hands. I'm surprised you've never noticed."

The Holy rolled his eyes. "Will you order one lit?"

"Of course," I said. "Scipio, light a fire."

With that, I turned from the bustle of the camp and went in search of my evening meal. It is in my nature— as with all foxes—to cache food supplies whenever and wherever possible. For voiceless foxes, the wherever is confined to their small territories. My territories have never been small.

I rounded the lake, the twins squabbling over the shell-fish they were pulling from the shallows fading in the distance. There was a clearing ahead where I had buried a pair of voles and the wing of a thrush, none of which should have rotted too much. But the scent I caught as I reached the edge of the cottonwoods did not rise from my cached food.

A thrill I had rarely experienced went through me. I knew before I saw her that a voiceless vixen was helping herself to the voles.

I crouched, chin on paws, and tuned my senses forward. Except for the initial scent, there was no sign of the interloper. If I had not been approaching from downwind, I might not have caught even that.

The direction of the wind was to my advantage, should a confrontation erupt. I was downslope, which meant she enjoyed the advantage of position. I was ignorant of her exact location, which mean she enjoyed the advantage of surprise. I was knowledgeable, which meant she enjoyed the advantage of ferocity.

I suppose one does not often think of foxes as ferocious. But any animal—particularly any voiceless animal— which depends upon the deaths of other creatures for its sustenance is possessed of anger and cunning, not just foxes.

Humans do not depend upon the deaths of animals, they simply choose to enjoy—if that's the word—the benefits of those deaths. Are humans ferocious? Is that the word?

I had let my mind wander. The vixen had not.

Suddenly, she was there, crouched low as I was. Her head cocked sideways in curiosity. She let forth a mewling noise that foxes, alone among the canids I had encountered, were capable of uttering.

I could startle her away by speaking. I could growl a threat. I could simply walk away. I would not be in danger should I choose any of those things. If I chose any of those things, I would learn nothing.

Since I first came to awareness on the Silver Road heading south toward Aquacolonia, I had encountered seven voiceless foxes in my travels, four of them cubs. Two of the adults had been vixens. It was the young I had studied the longest and approached the closest.

Until then. Until that day above the oxbow lake.

Voiceless foxes seemed to have an uncanny ability to sense and so avoid me. This vixen had chosen to approach instead of evade. For the moment, I forgot about Scipio Aemilanus and the ailing Empress, about Octavia Delphina and forcing her sister into Hell. Here was something fundamental to me, not to those I guided.

Her yellow eyes caught the sunset and flashed through red and orange and gold. She cocked her head the other direction but did not utter any other sound.

Aurochs can bellow in imitation of their voiceless kin, but the common wisdom is that it is simply that, an imitation. Loci and Foci often chittered to one another like voiceless raccoons, but once I asked them about it and they said it was a language of twins, not a language of the wild.

I had no way of communicating with this vixen. If foxes have a language, I do not know it.

She stood and turned, but she did not immediately walk away. She cocked her head over her shoulder and looked at me again. When she trotted up the hill into the clearing, I followed her.

Little mounds of loose earth dotted the field. My caches, all turned over. The vixen walked to the closest one and stuck her muzzle into the ground. She pulled the bird's wing free, set it beside the hole, and walked a short distance away. She lowered herself to the ground, watched me with her chin on her paws.

Gift giving? A peace offering? An apology for stealing my food?

There is a monograph on the behavior of foxes in the library for knowledgeable creatures outside Aquacolonia. I have studied it many times. I knew the mating and parenting habits of voiceless foxes. I knew their lifespans, which, like all the voiceless, were far shorter than knowledgeable creatures. I knew how and when and where they hunted. I knew where they denned.

None of the behaviors this vixen evinced had ever been recorded by any observer I was aware of, neither human nor knowledgeable creature.

What was this?

There was a sound of wind through feathers as a shadow dropped into the clearing between us. Malavus.

"Scipio orders you to return to the camp," she cawed, then immediately leapt into flight again.

When I looked back, the vixen was gone. The wing—a gift, an offering, an apology—lay where she had left it.

Tertius Decimus

THE SECOND JOURNEY

I RETURNED TO THE camp to find Scipio Aemilanus standing with his back to a sputtering smokey fire of green wood sticks. Perhaps he really had set it himself. His under priests were arrayed behind him in a half circle, the fire between them and their leader. One of them held a stout cudgel. Another rested his hand on a knife the length of a man's forearm at his belt. I had not noticed any weapons among their number earlier—they must have unpacked them from their bags while I was on the hill.

The Holies were facing Walks Along Woman, her two seconds, and a juvenile bison with a muddy coat tangled with thorns and dry leaves I had never seen before. Malavus was perched on a branch above, but the twins were nowhere to be seen.

"You sent for me, most Holy?" I asked, putting a bit of acid into it. I needed to know what was going on, which meant I needed time.

"This bull calf nearly killed me," Scipio Aemilanus said. "And now these northerners are threatening to quit the camp and deny us passage across their lands as well."

"The Holy exaggerates on all counts," said Walks Along Woman. "He is perhaps still frightened by my scout's sudden appearance, which nearly startled him into the fire."

I took the space between the two groups. "I am Quintus Shu'al," I said to the young bison. "I am the guide for this party."

"You are known to us," said the youngster, and his piping voice made him seem boyish. He was still well short of his full growth, his hump just starting to show.

"So I keep hearing," I said. "The Great Northern Membership has excellent sources of information, it seems."

"I am one of them," said the calf, more than a hint of pride tingeing his voice.

Walks Along Woman spoke. "I was interrupted in making my introductions by the . . . reaction of these Holies of the Hinge. It is just as well, as now you have returned, Quintus, I will not have to repeat myself."

The ambassador seemed like a person who did not like to repeat herself.

"This is Seems Dangerous," Walks Along Woman continued, indicating the calf. "He is the principal scout for the south-central borderlands, a great honor for one so young."

It was odd to hear this place, considerably north of Aquacolonia, described as being to the south.

Loci and Foci waddled into the clearing, their bellies

distended by one of their typically overzealous meals. Loci looked around, and said to his brother, "We should have stayed by the lake."

"No," said Foci. "Look who's here. The fiercest of all the Scouting Corps."

Seems Dangerous was moving his weight from side to side, a sign of excitement. "The mapmakers!" he said. "You live!"

Everyone turned and looked at the twins. At first, it seemed as if they were not going to respond to the youth. But then Loci said, "It's true. We're alive."

"But how? The cliffside! The cougar!" said Seems Dangerous.

"We're past that," said Foci.

"We're into metaphysics now," said Loci.

"Sealing the gates of Hell," said Foci.

"Ending death," said Loci.

This was an uncharacteristically verbose exchange for the twins. How they knew the scout was a mystery, but not one I was particularly interested in solving. I knew they traveled extensively without my guidance. I had been to places where they had preceded me.

"What is the meaning of this?" demanded Scipio.

"The meaning, Holy," said Walks Along Woman, "is simply that you have reached the border of the territory of the Great Northern Membership. You may address me as Ambassador no longer but Councilor. Before, when I judged you, it meant nothing but how annoyed I was with you. Now, my judgment counts for considerably more."

Scipio bristled. "You are to judge whether or not we may continue north?" he asked.

"I am to judge whether or not you live," said Walks Along Woman.

To his credit, the set of Scipio's jaw did not alter, and his next words rang with the confidence they usually did. "Threats, is it? What of the fabled deliberative processes of your Council? You would slaughter us on the border before I have the opportunity to present my case?"

Walks Along Woman laughed. "Well, I would prefer that," she said, "though it would be a selective slaughter. These cartographers are old friends of Seems Dangerous, and the crow would be difficult to catch."

I did not fail to note that I was not one of those she mentioned and so theoretically spared. Neither was Octavia Delphina.

"Do not worry, southerner," said the woman who had identified herself as a chief chosen by lots earlier. "I would not allow Walks Along Woman to hurt you. You have guest rights now."

"I don't see how you could stop her," muttered Scipio.

"I would simply order her to hold her peace," said the woman. "Unlike you, I can recognize when someone is making a joke."

"A porter, order an ambassador?" Scipio practically spat the words.

"She is no longer a porter," said Walks Along Woman. "She is the high chief of the southlands. I am not an ambassador. I am, as I already told you, a councilor. Councilors cannot overrule regional chiefs in their own lands, and she also outranks me by right of age."

It occurred to me I had no idea how long bison lived. I wondered if Walks Along Woman would tell me if I asked her.

"So, all this is a joke at my expense?" demanded Scipio.

"Yes," I said. "Surely your considerable honor and pride can survive such a light buffeting."

I turned to Seems Dangerous. "You look as if you have been in the field for some time. You are here to welcome us?"

"And to guide you the rest of the way. The Council has ruled you may not use the Silver Roads as you approach the Mootpoint."

Scipio started to say something at this revelation, but I raised a simple point first. "Do we carry enough food for all of us to make it that far?"

"Supplies will be brought," said the woman who was apparently the chief of the lands we had entered. "I have been told the Council will recompense us."

"And so we shall," said Walks Along Woman. Then she said, "I apologize, friend fox, for not telling you your services would be required in a more traditional manner for the final leg of our journey. You will guide us still?"

"I have never been to the Mootpoint," I said. The capital of the Great Northern Membership was famously hard for outsiders to track down. "But I can find it."

"Even if you had been," said Seems Dangerous, "the knowledge would not help you. The Mootpoint moves."

If I could have grinned at the calf I would have. "I can find it," I said again.

Quartus Decimus

THE FIRST JOURNEY

THE LADY OF TOOSA—or as I had learned to call her years before, simply Toosa—ordered her bear guards to stay outside the pavilion the people of the paramount chiefdom erected with admirable swiftness atop the nearby mound. She did not directly address either Cynthia Benedictus or me until we had been shown inside.

She sat on a cushion of rushes bound with leather strips. It didn't look particularly comfortable, but she had never been a woman I knew to seek out soft things. She gestured to the woven mats on the ground before her. I padded over, sat, and nodded to Cynthia Benedictus. The scholar took a seat beside me, crossing her legs before her.

"You have returned to us," said Toosa. Her leather vest, her cotton shirt, and her beaded skirt were all white, as was her headband and the string of her necklace of freshwater pearls. She had aged somewhat in the years since she had driven me from her lands, but no more so than the other humans of my acquaintance. She was still beautiful. She still looked strong.

"At some risk," said Cynthia Benedictus. "To hear him tell it."

"Yes," said Toosa, pursing her lips. "There is the matter of my sentencing you to death should you ever enter our lands again. The bears are quite eager to hear the outcome of this conversation."

"And what do you imagine that will be?" I asked.

Her lips curled in that knowing smile I had come to know so well.

"You will remember, Quintus, I have a rich imagination, but that it is bound by necessity. By tradition."

Cynthia Benedictus seemed remarkably unconcerned with this talk. She was looking around at Toosa's furnishings and cult objects. A large white vase etched in red showed a scene of two human skeletons being interred in a cairn. The tent had been pitched over a small tree. A carved wooden fox sat at Toosa's right hand.

"Your people evince a fascinating physical culture," Cynthia Benedictus said to Toosa.

The paramount chief turned to look at her other prisoner. Her other guest. I was having difficulty determining what she was planning.

"As do yours," said Toosa.

"And your command of the trade tongue is, well. It certainly matches my own."

"Is that what you call it?" asked Toosa. "A trade tongue. There are several trade tongues among the peoples of this continent. Remind me to tell you the story of when I met a delegation from the western mountains and there was a chain of four translators from communities all across the woodlands and plains between me and their ambassador."

"That *does* sound fascinating," said Cynthia Benedictus. "Were the negotiations successful?"

"I have no idea," said Toosa. "They seemed happy enough when they left, empty-handed. We never heard from them again. I'm quite sure the translators were busy making their own agreements and were happy for the hospitality and treasure we provided them for their services."

Cynthia Benedictus laughed. So did Toosa. I was beginning to get annoyed.

"Lady," I began, but Toosa held up her hand and shot me a warning look.

"In time, fox," she said.

Cynthia Benedictus looked between us. She swept her arm around the interior of the pavilion. "You keep three cults," she said.

Toosa looked impressed. "Blue said you were a scholar. Yes, your observation is correct. We keep the cult of death, which we will all know"—she indicated the vase—"and the cult of life, which we all live"—and here she nodded toward the tree. "And we keep the cult of animals, our kin and guides."

"Specifically, foxes," said Cynthia Benedictus, pointedly looking between the statue at Toosa's side and me.

"Sometimes foxes," said Toosa. "Today, foxes."

"I know that the keeping of cult among your people does not equate to worship. Or what we in the Empire call worship."

"You know much for a woman who has not been on this side of the ocean for very long."

Cynthia cocked her head. "How could you know how long I have been here?"

"Your people change the cadences of your tongues quickly, though you do not recognize it in yourselves. You do not speak like someone who has been in Aquacolonia for very long."

Except she did not say "Aquacolonia." She used a word I had heard her use before when discussing the port city, but which I had never managed to interpret to my satisfaction. It was something like "thorn."

"You must have a remarkably sensitive ear," said Cynthia Benedictus.

"And sight and touch and taste and smell as well," said Toosa, with no particular humility.

"Is this a quality you share with all your people?"

"Some of them," said Toosa. "The bears take great pride in their noses. The mammoths see better than most suspect."

"You count mammoths as your subjects?"

"If you like. 'Subject' is an . . . inexact word for our relationship."

I was growing restless.

"Settle, fox," said Toosa.

I did. I was in the position I had always found myself in with her. Without any footing.

"Do you mean the mammoths are knowledgeable? I have never heard of such."

"Those who live among the humans of this paramount chiefdom are knowledgeable. That is our law. You have never heard of such, you say. Until a short number of years ago, we had never heard of a knowledgeable fox."

The fur at the back of my neck stood up. I stood up, too.

"I have never known why you abandoned our friendship and drove me away under threat of death," I said. "If you mean to give me to your bears, just do it. But for whatever love you once held for me, please return this woman to her companions. She only set foot in your lands because I led her here."

"And why *did* you lead her here, Quintus?" I could not help but wonder why she had decided to finally use my name.

"It was an accident," I said. "A mistake."

"Some branching on the Silver Roads confused you?" She smiled again. She gestured for me to sit again.

I did not answer, but I sat.

"You knew this might happen," Cynthia Benedictus said to me. "You were . . . were you *counting* on it?"

Toosa looked as close to startled as I had ever seen her.

She tamped it down to simple curiosity before she spoke. "You play deep games, Quintus."

"I play no games," I said.

"What made you risk putting yourself in my hands?" Toosa asked.

"We need help. You are the only person I know capable of giving it."

"What do we need help for?" interrupted Cynthia Benedictus.

But Toosa was the one who answered her. "If this is the same fox who lived among us for two years," she said, "he must surely need our help keeping someone alive."

Cynthia turned her head, tossing it to keep her curls from falling across her eyes. "I thought it was *you* who were at risk of death."

"I am," I said. "Remember the bears?"

"You are not," said Toosa. "Remember the pronouncement?"

"What pronouncement?"

"The one I rendered that forced you from these forests and hills," she said.

"It boiled down to 'leave or die.' 'Come back and die.'"

"You show a remarkably unsubtle understanding of what I said," she replied. "It is most unlike you."

"I was in a bit of a hurry for subtleties," I said. "Why does everyone keep forgetting about the bears?"

Toosa stood, waving at us to remain seated. She spread

her arms and bowed her head for a moment. She raised her head, chin pointing at the deerskin ceiling. "Here are the words of the Lady of Toosa," she said. "Know this. The fox Quintus Shu'al has made for himself a home among us. He has dug dens near our villages and trod the game paths followed by the hunters. He has learned to sing our songs. Know this. Quintus Shu'al is to be held as an outsider from this day onward. He is no exile, because to be considered an exile is to acknowledge a kinship he does not possess. He is no prisoner, because we will not house and feed him should he be found again among us. He is to be driven out, and if he will not go, he will die."

There was a brief silence, then Cynthia Benedictus said, "In fairness to Quintus, that does sound a bit like leave or die."

"No," said Toosa. "It means to *stay* is death."

"More subtlety I don't understand?" I asked.

"Quintus. My dear friend and fellow student of the world. You cannot stay *anywhere* and live. You are a traveler and a guide. Navigators cannot live unless they are navigating."

I do not know how to describe the feeling that roused in me. What I said was, "Well."

To my surprise, Cynthia Benedictus had begun to cry.

Toosa looked from one of us to the other. "Of course I will help you," she said.

Quintus Decimus

THE SECOND JOURNEY

I LET THE BULL CALF, Seems Dangerous, lead us for a day or two until we were out of the low hills overlooking the rivers draining the middle of the continent. When we were well and truly into the endless plains, though, it soon became clear he was guiding us by guesswork and hope.

On the second evening in the grasslands, I approached him. "You have done well, Seems Dangerous," I said. "You have led us along the route I would have chosen exactly."

The calf looked at me mournfully. "The Mootpoint moves," he said, repeating what he had told me the day we met.

"Yes," I said. "But one of the great herds follows it, yes?" I had kept my ears sharp to the low conversations of the four northerners as we travelled. Their hope was that a party of outriders would stumble across us so we would be pointed in the direction we needed to be going. Walks Along Woman was confident we would catch up with the Mootpoint in good time, but time was something I didn't think Scipio Aemilanus would allow. Time was something I didn't know if I had.

"The councilor told me she is proud of me," said Seems Dangerous, perking up. "But I must admit to you, navigator, I do not know where to go next."

My eyes do not see the stars the same way those of humans are said to. I did not know whether bison could see the stars. For me, they are not pinpoints of light but pricking sensations on my nose and tongue. I smell the stars. I taste them. This is how I navigate off the road, by feeling stars.

And the stars, too, sense those of us in the terrestrial sphere. There is ever a movement in the net they cast, as if the motion of populations is like that of fish in a trawler's net, though much less frenzied.

I opened my mouth slightly and turned my head upward. I could feel a weight stretching the net to the north and the west. Not so close. Not so far. For now, it was resting, but there was a wake behind it, indicating a clear trend of motion.

"Will it do you a great dishonor if I lead us beginning in the morning?" I asked Seems Dangerous. "I can find the way."

"You know where to find the Mootpoint?" he asked me.

"I know *how* to find it," I said.

~

So it was on a day when there were no colors to be seen

but the browning green of the prairie grass and the intense blue of the cloudless sky that I trotted easily along before Walks Along Woman, Seems Dangerous, Octavia Delphina, Loci and Foci, and Scipio Aemilanus and the other Holies of the Hinge. Walks Along Woman still held out hope we would encounter a group of far-ranging guards riding out from the Mootpoint, but I was taking care to time our stops and modify our direction of travel so that would not be needed.

The travel was easy. Easy enough for Octavia Delphina to keep pace with me at the front.

"This is not the way you led my sister," she said after an hour of silence I had almost begun to think companionable.

I shook my head. "No," I said. "No, her destination was far to the east of here."

"I came with you to learn what happened to her, since you will not say."

"I thought," I said, "you came with us to exact some sort of revenge or in the hope of witnessing my death."

"Hope *is* eternal," she said.

The plains are not flat. We were at the top of a small rise. A smell even Octavia Delphina sensed blew up from along a small stream below us.

A wide track had flattened the grass, hundreds of spans across. Small mounds of manure pockmarked the sort-of road.

"Scipio!" I called back. "I think you can take the lead from here. Being the leader and all."

The Holy clicked his tongue and the horse he was riding dutifully moved up next to me. There was a slight curl to one side of his lip I did not like.

"Yes," he said. "These 'members' will see me first."

The various other Holies, mounted or on foot, moved past us, as did the northerners—Seems Dangerous giving me an appraising glance—and finally Loci and Foci. After being at the front, Octavia Delphina and I found ourselves shortly at the back.

"It is not that I will not tell you what happened on Cynthia's journey," I said, "it is that I cannot."

"Some great oath you swore?" she said, and her tone reminded me again she was not my friend.

"Some great ignorance I possess," I said. "I would tell you if I could. The reason I cannot is that I do not know your sister's fate."

Which was true, after a fashion.

~

One of the strangest experiences of my strange life was coming into the Mootpoint of the Great Northern Membership. It not only, as promised, moves, but it is in near *constant* motion.

Within a few hours of finding the herd's track, we saw

the trailing bison, humans, dogs, and mammoths making up the rear of the teeming mass of humans and knowledgeable and voiceless creatures that accompanied and surrounded the Mootpoint.

Dogs drew packs on travois, humans carried bundles on their heads or strapped to their backs, the mammoths were almost invisible beneath the bales and boxes tied to their flanks.

"I'll go ahead and make a path," said Seems Dangerous, and took off at a gallop before Scipio Aemilanus could raise the objection he clearly planned. Having failed to stop the young bison, he drew his horse to a halt and spoke to Walks Along Woman.

"When he returns, tell him I will meet the High Council of the Great Northern Membership here."

Walks Along Woman rumbled her laugh and kept walking. The two northern humans gave the Holy amused glances as they passed him by as well. Octavia Delphina shrugged and followed them, and Loci scrambled in her wake, leading the mule mounted by Foci. I waited with the under priests.

"Do you think they've gone to fetch the Council?" I asked Scipio.

He spat to one side. "Of course I don't think that. Here's another insult. We should let them go and return to the Silver Roads this instant."

I had no intention of guiding anyone onto the Silver

Roads, not while at the very heart of Great Northern Membership political power. Political and whatever other powers they possessed.

"Well, if you're not coming," I said, and stopped. "You know, Scipio? I really was just about to wish you luck. It's strange, isn't it, the habits polite society grinds into you." With that, I leapt forward, quickly reaching Walks Along Woman.

Seems Dangerous did his job well. The slow-moving herd—if that was the right word for so mixed a group of individuals—split before us like water around a rock in a stream. As we made our way through the cleared path, people called out to Walks Along Woman.

"Councilor! Welcome!"

"Walk wise, woman!" This was followed by a round of laughter.

There were also bellows from some of the bison. Were they voiceless? If they were, how did they recognize her? But too, dogs barked, and one mammoth let out a trumpet blast from her trunk. It was all very companionable.

"The Mootpoint is at the front of the herd?" I asked.

"No," said Walks Along Woman. "At the center."

"They send messengers to dictate direction and speed?"

"There are no dictates in the Membership, not from chief nor councilor. The herd is led by the grandfathers, and they keep their own counsel."

I considered this. "I look forward to learning more

about your people, Chief and Councilor," I said. "Perhaps we may speak after we meet with the Council."

"We may speak now," she replied. "It will be some time yet before we catch up to the Mootpoint."

"The herd is that large?"

"It is the largest assemblage of living creatures on the continent," she said. "Perhaps in all the world."

I remembered the tug of the stars and believed her.

~

The bull's name, or at least the one he shared with those of us from Aquacolonia, speaking the language of the Empire just as perfectly as Walks Along Woman, was Shattered Horn. Both of his curling horns were whole, though. He did not explain. Explanations in general were short in coming from the High Council of the Great Northern Membership.

In addition to Shattered Horn and Walks Along Woman, the High Council consisted of two human men and one human woman, the latter acting as translator for the former. Only Shattered Horn and Walks Along Woman seemed to speak any language I knew. A mammoth whose name was given as Little Ramage ambled along with the moving meeting, but never spoke. It was never clear if she was a member of the Council. Another bison cow besides Walks Along Woman rounded out the makeup. Her name was Fondness, and she was voiceless.

When he finally caught up with us and was apprised of the situation, Scipio Aemilanus took the opportunity of introductions to be insulted again. "This is just a beast," he said, upon learning Fondness' nature.

"You honor her," said Walks Along Woman.

Scipio Aemilanus had no immediate response.

"Messages have been sent us by our esteemed Walks Along Woman," said Shattered Horn, as if the Holy had said nothing—as if he were not there. When these messages could have been sent and who might have carried them was a mystery to me. I remembered our conversations about creatures that were supposedly impossible to make knowledgeable, and thought about the enormous variety of animals, insects, and birds that populated the plains country.

Shattered Horn went on. "You seek our permission to use the Silver Roads to cross the whole of our territory to the western Hell."

I had never heard the expression. Scipio looked sharp, then thoughtful.

"Permission, yes," I said. "And information if you can provide it."

"The Membership shares all it knows with any who ask," said Shattered Horn.

"At what price?" demanded Scipio.

Shattered Horn's laugh was lower than Walks Along Woman's. "We do not bargain for knowledge, though if you seek the western Hell, you will certainly pay a great price. But it will not be to us."

Loci and Foci had somehow both managed to cling to the top of the bundles their loping mule carried and had been busy with charcoal on a sheet of parchment. Before Scipio could make what I'm sure would have been a fruitless inquiry as to the nature of the supposed price of reaching our destination, the raccoons took a simultaneous and rather graceless leap from their mule to the ground, churned muddy by countless hooves and feet.

They trundled over to Fondness and, keeping pace with her, held up the sheet of paper. She swung her head toward them, swung it back forward. If the twins expected any more reaction, they did not show it. In fact, they seemed quite pleased.

"What do you have there, mapmakers?" asked Walks Along Woman.

Loci held up the sheet. It was a likeness of Fondness. It was one of the most beautiful drawings I had ever seen.

"She does not interpret images the way you do," Walks Along Woman said gently.

"We know this," the twins said, speaking atop one another. Their manner was an echo of the gnomic pronouncements of the Membership.

"Then why did you show it to her?" I asked, genuinely curious.

"Because we do not convey images the way you do," said Loci.

Or Foci. Their scents were obscured by the mass of creatures around us.

~

After the twins had tucked away their drawing, Scipio Aemilanus launched into a speech that, in so many, many words, amounted to a repetition of what Shattered Horn had already indicated the Membership well knew. He finished by saying, "And so, it is with these things in mind I implore you to grant us permission." His tone said something different. His tone said he intended to proceed with or without the consent of the High Council.

"We do not believe the end of death is a desirable outcome," said the human woman. She repeated herself in the language of the Membership and the two other human councilors nodded their agreement.

"But since neither do we believe such a thing is possible," said Shattered Horn, "we grant you what you believe to be your wish."

Scipio Aemilanus simply nodded and looked at me. The herd had at last stopped for the evening. Humans brought us wicker baskets full of boiled roots and dried berries. The baskets were tightly woven, but what made them especially beautiful were the geometric designs inked onto their broad handles.

"We should leave right now," said Scipio.

I shook my head like a human saying no.

"When?"

"The morning will be soon enough, Holy," said Walks Along Woman. "Do you not wish to enjoy our hospitality for a single night before you go off to meet death?"

"I am not going to meet death," said Scipio. "Death is a concept, not a person, not a place."

"I am curious as to how one ends a concept," she replied.

Scipio Aemilanus was standing next to the little fire of dried dung some humans of the Membership had built. Shadows and light played across his features. "By force," he said.

Sextus Decimus

THE SECOND JOURNEY

AT THE END OF the next day, when I stepped off the Roads I had to duck between the rear legs of the twins' mule. They had stopped stock-still.

Loci, leading the creature, turned and looked at me strangely. He pulled on the reins and walked over to where the Holies and Octavia Delphina were gathered, waiting for me to tell them what to do.

We were in tall grass prairie, but I had guided us to a patch of ground scorched clear by a lightning strike. Otherwise, the Holies would have had to stand on their saddles to see ahead, and the rest of us would have seen nothing but the bright green stalks.

The sky was low and white, neither sun nor moon visible. I had led the party longer than usual, and dark was coming on. Everyone was exhausted.

I put the under priests to work on a fire and a meal for the humans and raised my nose, trying to catch the scent of something I could make a repast of myself.

"What are you doing?"

Loci and Foci had somehow approached me without me hearing. For all that they were descended from and related to some of the stealthiest creatures of the animal kingdom, they had few skills in that direction themselves.

"Which one of you asked me that?" I said.

"I did," they said, simultaneously.

Something was awry. But I wasn't going to ask what.

"I am trying to decide if I have just caught scent of a chipmunk who must be very, very lost."

"We thought *you* were incapable of being lost," said Foci.

I lay down, put my chin on my front paws, waited them out.

"We do not know the way to the western Hell," said Loci.

"But it is surely not to the east," said his brother.

Found out on the very first night. I should have known it would be them. I had, in fact, entertained a notion that none of the humans would ever notice the direction of our course. Cartographers, though.

"There is a Hell in the east," I said, keeping my voice low. "It will serve the purposes of Scipio Aemilanus just as well as the one the Membership told him about."

"The Membership did not give us permission to travel east," said Foci.

"They put great store in permission," said Loci.

"None of the Membership are here," I said. "In fact, I

don't believe any of them to be within three days' walk."

The Council had spoken of sending a member of their Scouting Corps with us. I was glad Scipio had talked them out of it. I actually didn't know if Seems Dangerous would have intuited my deception quickly, but the same could not be said of the older scouts, humans or bison either one. And by all accounts, those veterans did not simply *seem* dangerous.

"What are you going to do?" I asked the twins. "Are you going to tell the Holies?"

This prompted a simultaneous click from back in their throats. It was their way of being dismissive.

"If the eastern Hell will serve just as well," Loci began.

"If so, why not strike for the western as was agreed?" Foci finished.

I did not answer.

"Ever a fox," said Loci and waddled away.

Foci lingered, so I asked him, "Can I still count you as allies?"

Again, the click.

"We were never your allies, Quintus," he said. "We are your friends."

~

The next day, as we walked the Silver Road, Scipio Aemilanus contrived to follow me when I had scouted ahead.

The others were far out of earshot.

"How much longer now?" he asked me, eagerness in his voice.

"Until what?" I replied.

His excitement at closing in on his goal must have cooled his temper, because instead of rising to my bait, he said, "Until we reach Hell."

I looked out into the argent mists either side of us, and ahead along the road that stretched so far it disappeared into a point, like an apprentice artist's perspective drawing.

"It's closer than you think," I said.

This time, it took him a visible effort to not let anger take him. "Not tonight, I think," he said. "But we travelled very far yesterday, and if you mean for us to have an easier day today as you told the scholar, we must be close."

I sighed. "We are close," I said.

It was an admission. It was even the truth.

~

"We are in the Eastern Woodlands," said Octavia Delphina matter-of-factly. The Holies were engaged in some sort of muttering ceremony and Loci and Foci had not returned from fishing at the stream at the bottom of the hollow. Octavia sat with her back against the trunk of a chestnut tree of such girth it would have taken seven or eight lanky men linking hands to encircle it.

"We are," I said.

"So, we are following my sister's route."

"No," I said. "But our route will reach her destination."

"The Hinge priests think we are heading west," she said. "Though how they can believe that in defiance of the evidence of their senses I do not know."

"The beliefs of Holies often run counter to the evidence of their senses."

She nodded, thoughtful. "That's true of some scholars as well," she said. "Not so navigators, I imagine."

Was she being *friendly*?

"I think if you asked any knowledgeable creature whether they depended more on their souls or their intellects the ones who would say their intellects would be the liars."

Septimus Decimus

THE FIRST JOURNEY

THE BEAR WHO SAW us into the hidden valley had refused to tell us his name. He had insisted we call him "the subcommander." He had left us at the top of the ridge we were descending just then.

"I wonder who the commander is," said Cynthia Benedictus, somehow making her way down a slope of shifting scree without any trouble. "Do you suppose the commander is a bear, too?"

"I don't know," I said, hopping from precarious position to precarious position on a route parallel to hers, hoping she wouldn't start a rockslide that would lead to the whole party scrambling for their lives.

"I bet it *is* another bear. An old gray bear who recites poetry."

"They don't call it poetry here," I said.

Cynthia Benedictus came to a halt. Well, to a very slow slide. "You mean the people of the paramount chiefdoms don't have poetry?"

"I mean they don't *call* it poetry. I mean I've never heard a word in any of their languages that would translate easily as poetry."

"But they have a tradition of verse? Of words rendered in a lovely or meaningful way?"

"Yes," I said. "To varying degrees. Keep moving."

She did keep moving. She also kept talking.

"So, when the Lady of Toosa was chanting there at the end, before they bundled us onto the longboats, was she reciting poetry, or something like poetry, or something that doesn't easily translate as poetry?"

"I told you I don't know the language she was speaking. To judge from what the subcommander told us I imagine it was something like 'get out, and never come back.'"

"You're moving up in her estimation," she replied. "Remember last time? Leave under threat of death?"

She had been chattering at me this way ever since the warriors of Toosa had moored the boats carrying our party upriver and offloaded our gear. They had promptly paddled away after we were ashore. I did not know how the bear was expected to return home.

We reached a long, low stone column leaned on its side. Cynthia took a seat there while the rest of the humans and knowledgeable creatures of the expedition finished making their way to the valley floor. They all carried heavy packs filled with instruments and journals and other accoutrements of a scientific expedition.

"This is a tree," said Cynthia as the others variously sat

and stretched, recovering from the descent.

There were poplars and various evergreens nearby, but she was patting her hand on the stone where she sat.

"That," I said, "is a boulder."

"A boulder shaped like a tree on its side?" she asked.

"A boulder of curious size and shape," I replied, hopping up to sit beside her.

"Look here," she said. "This is where a branch broke off when it fell." She pointed to a round bit of rock, protruding slightly from the main body of the boulder. Studying it closely, I saw its surface was made up of dozens and dozens of concentric circles.

"Someone carved that," I said.

Cynthia Benedictus was delighted. "There are Holies who would agree with you," she said. "The Green Goddess carved it, sure, if you like."

"How can a tree turn into a rock?" I asked.

"Not my area of expertise," she said. She stood and looked around. "But we are definitely entering country where my area of expertise will come into play."

"Medicine," I said. "You believe this is where you'll find the plants you need to cure the Empress of... of..." I trailed off. The specifics of whatever malady afflicted the Empress had never been part of the official communications about the Hundred Savants.

"Yes," she said. "If my theories are correct"—her tone told me how little credence she gave to the possibility her theories were *not* correct—"the geothermal activity in this valley will have infused certain succulents with a mixture of sulfur and brimstone that will yield a unique tisane with powerful healing properties."

"Succulents. The word the flower sellers use for cactus."

"Among other things, yes. But don't you worry. Get us past the geysers. My people know what they're looking for."

I considered the routing that would safely thread the geysers, sinks, pits of boiling clays, and springs giving off poisonous steams. It would have been one of my great accomplishments as a navigator if I had intended to attempt it.

It was midafternoon, but the sun was setting behind the high mountains to the west. The smell of smoke tinged with something like sulfur hung over the entire valley. The only direction to go was northwest, where the narrow defile we were in opened into a large flatland choked with trees and laced with streams and creeks.

"Time, then," I said.

Cynthia Benedictus reached down and ran her hand down my flank, stopping short of the base of my tail to pat my hip. It was perhaps the third or fourth time any human had ever touched me without permission. It was the second time a human touched me without permission and retracted their hand with all the fingers still attached.

"I know it's time, Quintus," she said.

And at that moment came a huge sound of sliding rock. A woman screamed and an ape pointed back the way we came. An enormous rhinoceros, shaggy red hair flying, razor-sharp horns gleaming, was charging down the slope straight at us.

"This way! This way!" I called, trying to be heard above the tumult of voices raised in fear. "Now! Come now! Run now!"

Cynthia Benedictus let out a high-pitched whistle and, in an instant, her whole band was running past in a double file, sharp and efficient as soldiers.

I split the columns, trusting Cynthia was following me. One of the humans shouted, "Why is it chasing us? I thought they avoided humans! Is it rabid?"

I did not answer.

Then the only sounds were ragged breath and footsteps, both coming fast. The expedition followed me on a curve around an area of steaming rock that looked as if it were blanching in a cook's pot. There was a line of trees to our right and some of the humans looked that way hopefully.

It was not hope that looked back.

Wild mastodons are among the most dangerous creatures on the continent. Left alone, they are placid herbivores, living in small herds making slow, circular migrations from grazing ground to grazing ground.

No one ever seems to leave them alone.

There were three of them. Their tusks were heavy with

brass rings and the hair around their eyes had been shaved. Copious amounts of blue dye spread there, none too carefully applied because it dripped down their cheeks, giving the impression their faces were engulfed in cool flames.

There was nothing cool about their demeanor.

In the past, when I had encountered mastodons bred for war, they had always been mounted, controlled by riders beholden to any one of various chiefdoms, usually nomadic in nature. Their inevitable first tactic was to simply trample their opponents underfoot, but if that failed, if their would-be victims were particularly fleet and managed to step aside, then came the great swings of the head, the thrusting and slashing with the filed-down tusks. No women or men rode these mastodons, but the great creatures seemed bent on using the same tactics.

Behind, the rhino bellowed another challenge. We had at least distanced it somewhat.

"This way!" I shouted. "Up onto the bluff!"

The blanched rock had risen on our left as we ran, and while I could still feel a heat in it, it was not so great it would scorch bare hands. The expedition climbed quickly, while the mastodons ran parallel to the ridge. They were not attacking us. They were herding us.

The ridge ran right up into the roots of the eastern mountains. The mastodons could not follow. But other things could. There was more movement in the tree line.

"What now?" asked Cynthia Benedictus, heaving to get

enough air. "And who is directing these creatures?"

"What does it matter?" I snapped. "It's clear someone doesn't want us here."

"If they don't want us here," Cynthia asked, "why are they driving us in instead of out?"

There was something unassailable about that. This time it *was* logic. Logic I had known she would deploy.

"I don't know," I said. "But I know a place where none of these beasts will follow."

"It's time," said Cynthia.

I didn't look at her. "I know it's time," I said.

~

A few hours later, the last of the expedition disappeared into the crack at the base of the cliff I had guided them to. Cynthia Benedictus had gone first, lighting the way with an oil lantern from her pack.

As the last explorer, a human man, stepped out of view, steam began rolling down from above. It was yellow and glowed with some internal luminescence. It fell in a curtain, spilling to the rocky ground in front of me, then seemed to bounce back up, a circular waterfall of noxious gas. It blocked any view of the crack Cynthia Benedictus and her followers had entered.

Malavus landed beside me.

"If you had asked me to tell you what a gateway to Hell

looked like," she said, "this is not what I would have described."

"I didn't ask you," I said.

"Ah, poor me," said the crow. "Nobody ever asks me anything. Just 'Fly here, Malavus,' and 'Carry this message, Malavus' and 'Shit on that senator, Malavus.'"

I did not turn to look at her. "Or, 'Make sure Quintus does as he's told, Malavus,'" I said.

"Why yes!" she said. "And imagine my surprise when you did!"

"Go to Hell, Malavus," I said. I pointed at the roiling curtain of yellow steam. "It's right there."

Duodevicensimus

THE SECOND JOURNEY

SCIPIO AEMILANUS SAT ON a boulder and watched his under priests set up a tent the size of a pavilion. We had only walked the Roads for a few hours that morning before I called the halt.

"We're here?" Scipio had asked.

"We're close enough," I had answered.

Until that day, the Holies had pitched relatively small tents, two priests assigned to each except for the more luxurious one reserved for their superior, who did not assemble his own shelter.

This was a much more elaborate affair. The fabric of it was dyed red and green, and they lifted a sort of lintel above the entrance that was gilded. I thought of the weight of all of it put together and spared a thought for their workhorses.

Octavia Delphina and the twins were ranged out along the little valley, going farther from the camp than I had advised. I had warned them about the geysers and other dangers and had to trust them. I knew there were no humans and few animals about.

"You are sitting on a tree," I said to Scipio Aemilanus.

He looked down at the long, low boulder. He didn't comment.

"We'll leave after the noon meal," he said. "The others will have the altar built and consecrated. It's within walking distance, you said?"

I had said so three times. I did not say so a fourth.

"The altar is on poles," he said. This was the first I had heard of any altar. "I brought four of my strongest brothers to carry it through the gates."

"Ah," I said. "Unless you can lift it yourself, I'm afraid it won't be making the trip."

"What?"

"You and I will be taking this final walk alone, Holy," I said. "The gates will not open for all of us."

"How could you possibly know that?" he demanded.

"No living human may pass the gates of Hell unaided," I said. "I am not a human, either living or dead. But I know how to open them. I opened them on your orders once already. And closed them again. You still have not fulfilled your part of the bargain that led to those actions, so if you wish to waste time and breath in argument, you may do so. Just finish before it's time to leave, and don't expect me to listen." I walked away.

I saw Octavia Delphina making her way back to camp. She was carrying an armful of flowers with blooms in the dying colors of the season.

"These are what she was looking for," she said, laying them carefully on the ground before me. "You brought her this far and then . . . then did whatever it is you did. Did she find these plants, at least?"

"She did not," I said. "And now I think you are guilty of maintaining a pretense. You are a very intelligent human. You must have guessed what happened to your sister and her companions."

"I still don't know why," she said.

I nodded toward the stone tree. "I led them in there," I said. "He sent them there."

"So my anger at you is misplaced?" She scoffed.

"No," I said. "It is simply incomplete."

"And now you—now *he*—is going to perform some ritual to seal the gates so that no one may ever pass them again? Do you believe *he* believes that possible? Is he insane?"

I thought about her questions. "I do not know if he believes it possible. Neither do I believe he is insane. I believe he has some plan I have not yet puzzled out, and I believe it is important I thwart it."

"You alone?"

"Me alone."

"No," she said.

~

Scipio wore the ridiculous attire of high ceremony on the Silver Roads. He had trouble keeping up, a combination of his unsuitable footwear—a pair of golden-winged talaria—and the length of his many nested skirts.

"You must walk more slowly," he said.

Octavia, in her simple trousers and boots, had no trouble keeping up, but nonetheless walked behind him.

"Must I?" I asked. "As in one of your ponderous processionals? I am not one of your under priests, Scipio."

"No one in all the Empire would ever mistake you for a Holy, Quintus."

True enough.

A moment later, he stopped completely. "What is that?" he asked, gesturing ahead.

"Still the Roads, Holy," I said.

"No," he said. "There's something different. There's . . . color."

Octavia walked up next to him. I had not told her what to expect during the long discussion that ultimately led to her accompanying us. "It looks like fire," she said.

"Yes," I said. "We are very close now."

I counted a thousand heartbeats before we reached the intersection.

Straight ahead, the Silver Road continued interminably. Crossing perpendicularly was a crimson path, just as wide, just as apparently endless. Instead of continuously shifting silver clouds, though, the boundaries of the way were flickering flames.

"You have never . . . I have read every word any scribe has ever recorded about your Silver Roads, and I have heard you speak of them for most of your life," said Scipio. "You have never mentioned anything like this."

"I've never seen anything like this," I said.

Octavia looked at me sharply.

"And yet you do not seem surprised," said Scipio.

"I have never seen it," I repeated. "But I knew it was here. I know what it is."

"And what is it?"

"This is the Red Road, Scipio Aemilanus."

"This is the way to Hell," said Octavia, her voice sure.

Scipio ignored her. "Malavus reported a physical entrance to Hell, a crack in a cliff."

"I did not say it is the only way," I replied.

"And why are we not going in that way?" he demanded.

"Because it is sealed. You know all about sealing gates to Hell, don't you? Would it count for much if they could be opened again once they were closed?"

Suddenly, he gathered up his skirts and looked left and right.

"Which way?" he asked.

"Either will work," I said.

He took the sinister route, and I had to trot to catch up with him. Once again, Octavia took up the rear.

"I am not going to seal any gates," he muttered, almost

as if to himself. He looked down at me, though he did not break stride. "End death? You think me mad?"

I did not reply. The overpowering sense I was about to learn something important hung there.

"Cynthia Benedictus would never have found a cure for the Empress, even if my methods had not required the sacrifice of her and her expedition."

"She seemed a very able woman," I said.

"Not able enough to raise the dead," Scipio said.

What? But I did not reply aloud.

"I see," said Octavia. "My sister's life for hers. Cynthia's life and those of her companions."

"Quintus, you never suspected. Nobody ever suspected. None of you millions and millions." He was talking faster and faster. "She is dead, fox. The Empress died six years ago."

I shook my head. "Then why are we here?"

"Because I was the one chosen among the keepers of the imperial tradition to come here. I was the one chosen to bring the Empress back from beyond Hell's gates."

"For the dead, the gates of Hell are one-way," I said.

"No gate is one-way," Scipio said.

No. No gate is.

Undevicensimus

THE SECOND JOURNEY

THE FIRST THING Scipio Aemilanus saw when he stepped off the Red Road was the shade of the Empress, her skin and hair and raiment a white so chill it glowed blue.

The first thing Octavia Delphina saw was Cynthia Benedictus, stretched out on the cavern floor before the entrance to a deeper cave, making herself comfortable on a bundle of travel goods.

"Why are you here already?" Cynthia Benedictus asked, looking at me. Then she saw her sister and scrambled to her feet.

Scipio said, "Blessed Empress, oh! Blessed Empress, I have come to lead you to renaissance!"

"I have missed you more than I can say," Cynthia said to her sister. She pointed up at the floating ghost. "Also, turns out the Empress is dead."

I looked from ghost to Holy to the scholarly sisters, trying to understand the situation.

Octavia asked, "What do you mean 'already'? It's

been over a year."

"Please, Empress, speak!" shouted Scipio.

The Empress did not speak. Blue light shone from her eyes. Her clothing seemed stirred by air currents not otherwise detectable.

"It hasn't been more than a day," said Cynthia Benedictus. "Unless . . . have any of your philosophers told you about subjective time?"

"I can guess what it means," I said. "It makes me wonder how long will have passed when we leave."

"We're leaving already?" asked Cynthia. "What about him?"

Scipio Aemilanus was positively rapturous, holding his arms wide. His eyes were closed, sweat rolled down his forehead, his mouth was open. He looked like the zealot I had always thought he was just pretending to be.

"Well?" asked Octavia.

"I was just considering," I said, addressing her sister. "You and Toosa left his fate to me. I'm thinking of leaving him here."

"Who is Toosa?" asked Octavia.

Scipio was paying closer attention to us than I had thought, though. "No!" he shouted. "You will open the way! I will lead the Empress forth in glory!" He slid, of all things, a fisherman's boning knife from his sleeve.

This was not the man I had known for so long.

"Settle yourself, Scipio," I said. "You have secrets to reveal yet, and you have a little bargaining power. Not so much as me, but a little."

"Quintus . . ." said Cynthia Benedictus. Octavia put her hand on her sister's shoulder and nodded her assent at the unvoiced concern.

"No, friends," I told her. "You know the whys of all of this. I would know the hows. I would know the whos."

"And I am the one who can tell you," said Scipio Aemilanus, something of his normal demeanor returning.

The Empress wailed. The sound was so loud, it felt like a physical blow. Scipio Aemilanus and the sisters covered their ears with their hands, and mine folded back of their own accord.

I slipped in the sudden cold. A patina of ice covered everything within view.

"That's the third time she's done that," said Cynthia Benedictus, shaking her head as if trying to dislodge something stuck to her scalp. "The ice is new, though."

"Tell me, scholar," demanded Scipio Aemilanus, "has she spoken?"

"My experience of the dead is limited, Aemilanus"— and he did not react to the insult of being addressed in this way—"but from what I've seen, the dead are not overly communicative. In fact, the few we've seen seem to be absent any cognitive faculties."

"She will revive under the light of the sun she commands!" he shouted, the fanaticism back in full force.

"Quintus Shu'al! Open the way! Lead us into the living world and I will tell you all you want to know and more, should she allow it!"

Should she allow it. This was not a clause in our contract. But then, I had violated the contract myself in leaving Cynthia Benedictus and her companions alive and, to all appearances, well.

"Tell me who made me," I said. "And I will open the way."

Scipio looked from me to the blank-faced apparition. Back at me, back at her. "What is your will, Empress?"

"Please don't encourage her to speak," said Cynthia Benedictus.

But the ghost's only response was to slowly rotate, to lean forward and backward. Her slippered feet hung above the cavern floor at the height of Scipio's eyes. She was trying to move. Trying and failing. Was she bound?

"Cynthia," I said. "Call your companions. I am going to send them onto the Roads while the Holy and I negotiate."

Scipio seemed not to hear this. He was studying the motions of the figure he was, to my mind, treating as a goddess. Where was the God of the Hinge in this? What door was swinging, according to Scipio's theology? What *gate*?

Cynthia nodded and let out a high whistle. Within a few heartbeats, a clear-eyed weasel whose name I had forgotten loped out of the cavern behind her. He peered at me, winced at the sight of the ghastly, dancing Empress, and said, "Already?"

"Already," said Cynthia Benedictus. "And make haste."

The line of humans and knowledgeable creatures I let onto the Red Road did, in fact, move quickly. "Stay still once you're through," I told them. "We will join you soon."

I hoped that was true.

I looked at Cynthia Benedictus and Octavia Delphina. "Well? I cannot hold the way open indefinitely. Go."

Cynthia smiled the version of her smile that called me a fool. "I'll go when you do," she said. "There's a paramount chief dressed all in white I promised I'd keep you alive. And unlike you and this Holy, I am a keeper of promises."

"I have not broken any promises to you. Or to Toosa, for that matter."

"I'm making allowances," she said.

Octavia had been watching the Holy. "We'll go together," she said. "And it had best be soon."

"She is stuck!" cried Scipio Aemilanus. "There is some force preventing her from moving!" He rounded on me. "Do something!"

I nodded once at the sisters and moved to stand next to the Holy, who I was increasingly convinced had completely lost his mind.

"Do something!" he shouted.

"I do not think it is in my power to free a dead soul from Hell, Scipio," I said. "I do not have the knowledge. I do not have the wisdom. Those are things within your remit, not mine."

Surprising me, he nodded. "Yes. Yes! It is within *my* power to pull her free!" He hesitated, confusion appearing on his flushed face. He was working up to something, gathering courage.

"Wait," I said. "First, you must answer my questions!"

"I have," he said, throwing his shoulders back and letting the knife clatter down. "I long since have."

"You haven't! I don't know! I don't know!"

He reached up and grasped the Empress by her ankles.

I had not thought it possible she could scream more loudly, but she did. Blood flowed from my ears and the sisters collapsed unconscious in the battering noise.

This time, the ice that appeared was like great gloves around Scipio Aemilanus' hands and wrists. It spread down his arms, over his shoulders, and down his torso, and fixed his legs to the ground. Again, the light of fanaticism was in his eyes, and it stayed there as the ice swallowed him whole.

At last, the scream stopped.

I shuddered in the sudden silence. Cynthia moaned but did not rouse herself. Octavia raised herself up into a sitting position, leaning on her hands. The temperature in the cavern was rising perceptibly, not just to the level it had been before the freezing scream, but hotter.

The icy statue that had been Scipio Aemilanus did not

weep. It showed no signs of melting, despite the ambient temperature becoming uncomfortably, dangerously hot.

The Empress of the known world, or something Scipio Aemilanus had believed was her, looked down at me. Her robes no longer flowed, and the penumbra of blue light around her was dying. No, not dying, *changing*. It was shifting from blue through green, into yellow.

"Octavia," I shouted. "Rouse your sister!"

Octavia crawled over to Cynthia and shook her shoulder. Nothing. Then, surprising me, she smacked Cynthia hard, and both sisters were instantly on their feet.

"Come," I told them.

Cynthia shook her head. "I cannot hear!" she shouted.

I looked across the room to where the members of her expedition had stepped onto the Red Road, and she must have understood, because she staggered to her feet and stumbled across the cavern, she and her sister leaning upon one another. Neither of them spared so much as a glance for the revenant, now flowing crimson, or the invulnerable statue of ice.

I did. I gave them one last look, thinking of everything I had learned. Thinking of everything I remained ignorant of. Would I ever know who made me?

Then I navigated out of Hell.

Vicensimus

ON THE JOURNEY BACK to Aquacolonia, Octavia Delphina and Cynthia Benedictus spent hours in conversation with one another about what was likely to happen in the Empire once the truth of the death of the Empress—and the truth of the conspiracy that had kept that knowledge from the citizenry—was revealed.

I did not involve myself in their speculation. I did not know. I did not care. Would fire and tumult come to this continent? Frankly, it seemed unlikely to me. The Empire had only a toehold here, not the firm grasp it held in other places. The so-called middle of the world might very well burn, but I did not believe then—I do not believe now—that anything more than ashes from any such conflict will ever settle here. The Empire seems farther away now than it ever has, and I am not alone in feeling that way.

Our trip home—home, there's a word—offered us two options. To stay to the east and head south through the territory of the Lady of Toosa, or to return through the lands of the Great Northern Membership. The sisters believed we owed each nation explanations and, perhaps, obeisances. I told them to decide, and I would guide them through whatever lands they wanted.

In the end, it was decided that both the Lady of Toosa and the High Council of the Great Northern Membership deserved to know what the imperials would learn later. So, Loci and Foci and a number of Cynthia Benedictus' colleagues from the first journey went overland to find Walks Along Woman and Shattered Horn and all their number, while I led the sisters and the rest of the Benedictus Expedition back to Toosa, almost due south from the steamy valley.

I have not spoken of the other Holies, of the under priests Scipio Aemilanus had dragged, in seeming ignorance, along his mad journey. They had been first defiant, then dazed, when told their master would not be returning from beyond the gates of Hell. I do not now think any one of them truly believed Scipio's stated purpose was his real one, but I never heard any one of them question it, either. They perceived the journey, apparently, as a failure. In any case, they elected to travel south on their own, steering a course between the sisters and me on the Roads and the route the twins took to the west.

They were never heard from again. It is not wise to venture through the interior of this continent, ignorant of any language or the customs of any people, on the Silver

Roads or not, without the services of a navigator. Or at least of a pair of cartographers.

Toosa welcomed us with great ceremony. We lingered in her territory for longer than I would have liked—the pain of the Lady's revelation that I could never stay there, that the Roads were my only home, was too fresh—but not so long as Cynthia Benedictus would have liked. The scholar has since returned to Toosa, accompanying members of the embassy from that paramount chiefdom who arrived in Aquacolonia shortly after we returned, the first such official contact that had been made between those people and the imperial colony.

Loci and Foci did not return to the city, either. They sent word they were striking west with a few bison of the Membership. The only hint of their destination was in a scrawled note included with their papers and maps, which they sent directly to me, care of the Sodality. We *will return from the east.*

Racoons.

Now, all the people whose lives were disrupted by the machinations of Scipio Aemilanus—and, it must be said, by the machinations of myself—are accounted for except for three.

I have not seen Malavus again. I wonder sometimes if she has seen me.

The second person is the scholar Octavia Delphina, who now holds great sway in the Sodality of Explorers and in the relations the city is building with the people of this continent, as word from across the great ocean grows more infrequent and more troubling. I see her often. She has taken to calling me her "domestic advisor," a title I neither want nor deserve, domesticity not being something I have much knowledge of.

And there is me.

I came into awareness in another world, on the Silver Roads. I have lived the intervening years stepping between them and this world, the supposed "real" world. I have been tested and tried along the Roads, on the plains and in the mountains of this continent, and in Hell. I do not know if Hell can be called a world. I do not know if it can be called a place.

My origins have been the great central mystery of my life. Octavia Delphina has told me I should abandon any thought of learning them. "You lack precedent, Quintus," she said. "That is not such a bad thing."

And yet, and yet, and yet. I am still unmoored. Unlike whatever remnant of the Empress we encountered beyond the Red Road, I am unstuck.

I remain ignorant of myself in fundamental ways I cannot correct. With the death of Scipio Aemilanus—if it was his death—the only avenue to the truth I had ever uncovered was lost.

"How do you know Scipio knew the truth, Quintus?"

Three women have posed this question to me at one

time or another. I have never tried to answer them.

I remain a mystery to myself.

I remain an outlier and an unknown quantity at best, and a liar and a rogue at worst.

I remain, still, somehow, Quintus.

I remain the only navigating fox.

About the Author

© 2022 Gwenda Bond

CHRISTOPHER ROWE is the author of the acclaimed story collection *Telling the Map*, as well as a middle grade series, The Supernormal Sleuthing Service, cowritten with his wife, author Gwenda Bond. He has been a finalist for the Hugo, Nebula, World Fantasy, Neukom, and Theodore Sturgeon Awards. He lives in a hundred-year-old house in Lexington, Kentucky, with his wife and their many unruly pets.

TOR·COM

Science fiction. Fantasy. The universe.

And related subjects.

*

More than just a publisher's website, *Tor.com*
is a venue for **original fiction, comics,** and
discussion of the entire field of SF and fantasy,
in all media and from all sources. Visit our site
today—and join the conversation yourself.